Rune

A Doyle Witch Mystery Prequel
Kirsten Weiss

misterio press

About the Book

IN THE SHADOWED SIERRA town of Doyle, Lenore hides from a world she distrusts, seeking solace in books to escape the visions she denies. But when she finds a man's body in Doyle Creek and her beloved aunt becomes a target of suspicion, Lenore is drawn into a web of small-town secrets and old grudges.

Pursuing a killer, she risks unraveling Doyle's enchanted core. Can Lenore, long wary of her shamanic gifts, embrace her magic to save herself?

Step into *Rune*, a captivating Doyle Witch prequel novella. Get cozy with this witch mystery now, and uncover the mysteries of Lenore's mystical past.

Poem spell in the back of the book!

Contents

Special Offer!

THANK YOU FOR BUYING *Rune*! I have a free gift if you'd like to have some witchy fun! You can join the Kitchen Witch Course, FREE right here —> Take the Challenge!https://www.kirstenweiss.com/kitchen-witch-challenge

The Witches of Doyle are amateur detectives and practical witches. So I'm offering this free gift: a 5-day email course in kitchen witchery.

For five days, you'll receive a fresh email in your inbox with a lesson and a quick assignment (each no more than 15 minutes long, because I know how busy you are). There will be spells, recipes, recipes for spells... Did I mention it's free?

So get in it, get on it, and invite a friend!

Copyright

Visit the author website to sign up for updates on upcoming books and fun, free stuff: KirstenWeiss.com

Chapter 1

I WAS TWENTY-FIVE WHEN I learned you can't pretend away who you are. Pretending only makes it worse when reality finally catches up with you.

Reality always catches up. And I say that today as a shamanic witch—someone who regularly engages in magical thinking.

I wasn't a witch back then though—socially awkward and fighting my magic every step of the way. But even today, I can't entirely blame my youthful self's resistance to my calling.

Whoever coined the phrase "unquiet dead" knew what they were talking about. The dead are far from silent. Ghosts ramble and rove, digress and drift, babble and blather.

Their thoughts are scattered, splintered, shattered. If ghosts were logical, they probably wouldn't be stuck in middle world, our world.

It was one of the many reasons why my twenty-five-year-old self avoided them. But I was in avoidance mode for other reasons that June day.

I strode stiffly down the serpentine trail. Morning sunlight drifted through cinnamon-barked Ponderosa pines. A warm breeze soughed in the branches.

I glanced up the hillside on my right. Snow still dotted its clefts and crannies as well as the shade beneath the trees. Last winter had been ferocious. Its remnants still lingered.

The murmur of Doyle creek grew louder in the valley beneath. Leaving the trail, I picked my way down the hill, my canvas-colored trail runners slipping on loose earth.

I wound around pale granite boulders toward the water. Finally, I emerged on a strip of sandy shore, no more than ten feet long and three feet wide.

Sierra snow melt ripped past the modest swimming hole sheltered by granite stones. But I wasn't here to swim. The water would be freezing. I was here to escape.

Setting down my canvas pack, I dug out a pen, a notebook, and my tattered copy of *The Two Towers*. I waited to see what urge would take me—to read or to write.

No, *not to write*. Feeling sorry for myself was never the best state of mind for writing. It led to self-indulgent sappiness.

Returning pen and notebook to my pack, I readjusted the elastic band around my blond hair and reapplied my sunscreen—a necessity when you're fair skinned. I opened my paperback.

For once, I did not get lost in Tolkien's world of hobbits and elves. Our Aunt Ellen had been right, and I wasn't happy about it.

A corner of my mouth angled upward. I was never happy when I was wrong. Given all the practice I'd had at being wrong, I should have been used to it by now. My gaze flicked skyward. A hawk screamed a laugh in the blue sky.

Aunt Ellen had raised my sisters and me after the death of our parents. For reasons known only to Ellen (since most sensible people believed magic wasn't real), our guardian had trained us in the basics of magic—but only the basics. Magic didn't come naturally to Ellen as it did to Jayce and me.

Our sister Karin struggled with it too. Maybe that was why Karin was the closest of us triplets to our aunt. Ellen had *worked* for her magic. She'd studied, and she'd struggled. Karin was still struggling.

I bent to reread the page I'd skimmed without seeing. My neck corded. I didn't have to work to see dead people. The dead were simply... there.

And that was a problem. I shifted, cold sand crunching beneath my lightweight khaki hiking slacks.

It wasn't that I didn't sympathize with the ghosts. I *wanted* to ease their pain and send them to the light like the mediums on TV. But it was never as easy as it looked on TV.

Which had led to our latest argument. Ellen was becoming a broken record on the subject.

Avoidance never works, Lenore. Finish your mediumship training. Finish something—that bookcase for starters. And get a real job in the real world with real people, while you're at it.

I closed the paperback. I *had* a real job, thank you very much, editing books written by financial advisors. It let me work from home. The pay wasn't great, but it was work.

And I didn't *want* to be a medium. Ellen seemed to think I was just trying to get out of walking my path, whatever that was.

I thought I should get a say in what path I took. Ellen had chosen hers. Why couldn't I?

I really should finish building that bookcase though. Leaning back, I braced my elbows in the sand, still damp from last night's rain. I stretched out my legs, crossing them at the ankles.

Something shifted in a fresh puddle beneath a cream-colored granite boulder. I leaned forward for a better look. A dragonfly struggled in the puddle, its mercury wings waterlogged.

Crouching, I studied the insect, its body striped silvery blue. I scooped up water and dragonfly together. Careful not to damage its delicate wings, I let the water drain from my palms.

The dragonfly collapsed in my hand, its wings drooping. My breath caught. Had I been too late? Too ungentle?

Its iridescent wings flapped slowly, and I exhaled. I stayed there, crouched and unmoving, until my knees ached. Then the dragonfly lifted from my hands and zoomed off, low over the swimming hole, and crossed the burbling creek.

Straightening, I watched the fast-running water splash past the sheltered swimming hole. I grabbed my canvas pack and jammed it behind my head for a pillow.

Neither reading nor writing was happening today. My brain was too busy spinning in circles. I relaxed my body, weaving the sound of the creek into daydreams of fantasy lands.

Something white flashed past in the stream, and I sat up, frowning. Another flash of white rippled past, and then another.

I rose and walked to the water's edge. Three more white things the size and shape of business cards floated past.

One spiraled into the swimming hole. Dampened by water, the paper was too shiny and stiff for a business card. A black symbol decorated one side, and I puckered my forehead. A rune?

My aunt had a set, but runes weren't my specialty. I knew they came from the Norse, and each was believed to hold a symbolic meaning, making them useful for divination. That was where my knowledge ended.

The white paper shot from the swimming hole and into the creek. More floated past.

Curious now, I scrambled onto a boulder overlooking the rushing water. A trio of the white things floated toward me. I stretched out one hand. They drifted past, just out of reach.

I lay on my belly, catching the toe of my hiking boot in a divot in the warm stone, anchoring me, my chest above the water. Another piece of stiff paper floated toward me, too far away to grasp.

Releasing my anchor, I scootched further out on the boulder, my midsection over the creek. I wobbled, stretching, and snatched the card from the freezing water. My body lurched downward.

I slapped my free hand on the stone beneath me, halting my fall. The creek rushed inches beneath my nose. Slowly, I exhaled. I looked up, bracing my muscles to lever myself up and backwards.

But I did none of those things.

Instead, I looked into the face of a dead man.

Chapter 2

THE MAN WAS DEAD, and he wasn't a ghost.

I shrieked. My muscles loosened from the shock, and I nearly tipped into the creek again. The sound of my cry echoed off the granite boulders and was absorbed into the rushing water.

The man's head bobbed sickeningly in the creek. His lips were blue, his skin waxy and battered, his brown eyes open and cloudy. His bare flesh was scraped and raw.

My heart rabbited. His body wasn't moving past with the current. It must have caught on something—a piece of wood, a stone.

I scrambled backward on the boulder, my chest heaving. *Dead.* He was dead.

Observe don't absorb. Observe don't absorb. It was one of Ellen's favorite sayings whenever I saw a ghost. It meant to notice, to see, but not to take it in.

The quickest way not to focus on the bad was to distract myself. I focused on the faint breeze on my face, on its waterlike sound through the pines, on how good it felt on my skin. The exercise slowed my racing pulse.

I fumbled for my phone and discovered I was still holding the rune paper, which wasn't paper at all. It was a sticker.

Jamming the sticker roughly into the rear pocket of my slacks, I retreated over the boulders to shore. I pulled my phone from one of the many pockets in my pale khakis. *No signal.* I shook my head.

I grimaced. If I left the man's body, it might continue downstream. But I'd *have* to leave the body if I wanted to get help.

Slinging my pack over one shoulder, I hiked uphill to the trail. I checked my phone. *Still no signal.* I huffed and scrubbed my free hand over my face.

I retreated farther down the path, phone in the air. Thirty minutes later, I descended into the parking lot where my used gray Volvo waited. And finally, I got a signal.

I called nine-one-one and explained. My breathlessness wasn't entirely due to the hike. *Observe, don't absorb.*

"Officers and paramedics are on their way," the dispatcher said. "They'll be there soon. Can you see or hear anyone else in the parking lot?"

My pulse skittered. "No." I hadn't considered I might be in danger until she'd brought it up, and I scanned the pines edging the lot. The shadows beneath them darkened.

A hawk gracefully descended from the sky. The bird landed on a pine branch above a seventies-era VW van complete with flowers painted on its yellow sides.

"Okay, Lenore, stay where you are, and keep me updated if anything changes. Help is almost there. Wait in your car and lock the doors."

"I will." I slid hurriedly inside my car.

The dispatcher disconnected. Disbelieving, I stared at my phone. She'd hung up on me? Now?

I shook myself. Dropped calls weren't unusual in the mountains. It hadn't been intentional, and it wasn't a harbinger of doom.

Even if she'd stayed with me, there wasn't much she could do if a killer complete with chainsaw and hockey mask stepped from the pines.

Could chainsaws cut through Volvos? I locked the doors. I gripped the phone.

I stared at the only other vehicle in the lot—the van. A *Save the Whales* sticker had been plastered on its back bumper, and I sucked in a breath. *Abe Crowe's van.*

That had been Abe Crowe in the river. I'd told the dispatcher I hadn't recognized the man, and I hadn't at the time. Our local environmental gadfly had looked so *wrong*, his ruined face battered and gray.

But that hadn't been what had thrown off my identification. *He'd* been gone. I hadn't recognized the body without the animation of his soul.

From his perch in the pine tree, the hawk eyed my Volvo. I tugged at the collar of my tunic. The bird was a handsome fellow with a red tail, but his steady regard made me uneasy.

I returned my attention to the van. *Stay in the car.* I drummed my fingers on the wheel. *Stay in the car.* I glanced back at the trailhead, bracketed by two stones like battleships.

"Fine, I'll *stay* in the car." I started the Volvo and edged closer to the van, stopping fifteen feet away. I circled the van. There was no bloody tire iron, no rain dampened note on the windshield, no obvious indicator of what had happened.

But the driver's side window had been smashed. Twin footprints marred the damp earth beneath it. I drove closer.

Rolling down my window, I leaned out for a better view. The van was too far to see the tracks well though, and I didn't dare get closer. What if I accidentally destroyed evidence?

I stuck my phone out the window, zoomed in and took a picture. I studied the photo on my screen. The waterlogged tracks were wide and the treads still deep, like Abe had dropped heavily from the van to the soft earth.

Head out the window, I completed my circuit around the van. A scattering of wooden matchsticks lay in a pile close to the edge of the parking lot.

The ground was slightly paler beneath the van than the dark earth surrounding it. Abe's van must have spent the night here. It had rained last night—though not enough to destroy the footprints—and I'd seen Abe in town yesterday afternoon.

He'd been loading groceries into the back of his van with the help of Doyle's latest odd-jobs man, Jonas.

A movement near the van drew my gaze. A lanky man, roughly my age, in his mid-twenties had sidled around the corner of the yellow van.

No hockey mask. No chainsaw. His thick coffee hair brushed the collar of a threadbare denim jacket. I sagged against my seat back.

"Jonas?" I called out, uncertain. Jonas was a loner and recent arrival to the town of Doyle. We'd never spoken, but there were a depressing number of Doyle citizens I hadn't said more than a few words to.

"Is Wharton with you?" he shouted.

Wharton? I ran my hands over my hair. "No," I said, "it's Abe. He's dead. He—"

Jonas bolted into the woods.

"Thanks a lot," I muttered. It wasn't as if I was going to recruit him to pull the body from the creek.

So why *had* I called out to him?

I shivered, though the late morning air was warm, and cranked up my window. *Company.* I'd called because I'd craved simple, living human company, though I'd always thought I was a contented introvert. "So that's a first," I muttered.

It took another thirty minutes for the sheriff's deputies to arrive. A fire truck and ambulance followed close behind, filling the lot.

When it became clear none of the deputies knew about the little beach, I led the men down the trail. We tramped quickly, single file.

Deputy Denton interrogated me from two paces behind. Owen was Pacific-eyed California gold, an ex-football player, broad of shoulder, blond of hair, trim of waist. In high school, all the girls had sighed over him—even me, and I'd been homeschooled.

A part of me was flattered by his interest now, even though it was all business. So I guess I *still* had a crush on him. I hoped he didn't realize my blushes and stammers were because of it, because he was laughably out of my league.

No, I hadn't seen anyone on the trail, but Jonas had been in the parking lot. Yes, I had recognized the dead man, belatedly—Abe Crowe. "Only because I recognized his van."

"Crowe?" Owen Denton stopped short and pointed at a redheaded deputy. "Go back to the lot. Secure the van."

The deputy nodded and hurried back down the trail.

Denton motioned me onward. "I should have guessed. I know Crowe's van too well. I helped him break into it last week again. He can't stop locking his keys inside."

"Again?" I rubbed absently at my arms. I'd locked my keys in Ellen's old car once as a teenager and had learned my lesson. Now that I had a newer car, I kept the fob in my pocket.

"His ex-wife took their new car with the keyless fob to Florida. When Abe had to go back to using the manual key for that old van... He just kept forgetting."

And I was focusing on unimportant details to keep from thinking of the body. "Where's the sheriff?" I asked. "Is she coming?"

"She's, uh, out of town today."

I turned. The deputy's face had reddened.

"Because of her husband," he continued. "You know?"

My face warmed. I knew. *Everyone* knew. The sheriff's husband had been caught running a welfare scam. He worked for the county government, so he'd been well placed to commit the fraud.

We reached the creek's thin strip of beach. I pointed. "He's on the other side of that boulder. Or he was."

Lightly, I touched my throat, my chest tightening. The water was running fast. Would the body still be there? Had I left Abe's corpse only for it to be swept away?

One of the deputies scrambled onto the boulder and vanished. Water splashed. "Got him," he shouted.

Thank God. I pressed my palms to my eyes, relieved.

"Thanks, Lenore," Denton said. "You can go home now. If we have more questions, we know where to find you."

I hesitated. But this was none of my business. It was time to retreat.

"Thanks." I nodded, turned, froze.

Abe's ghost crouched on the strip of sand in jeans and a forest-green jacket. His graying hair was thick and tufted. His eyes crackled with fury. The ghost charged, his phantasmic form rippling through me, and I inhaled an arctic scream.

Chapter 3

THE COLD WAS SHOCKING.

It wasn't the cold of fresh snowmelt—that would have been preferable. It was the cold of the dead, the cold of a morgue. It was the cold of annihilation, of despair, of loneliness. Cold clutched my throat and forced out a gasp.

The ghost was through me in seconds, leaving my teeth chattering. But like a big earthquake, each second in it had seemed a minute.

"Something wrong?" Denton asked.

Abe's ghost spun. It flailed on top of the swimming hole's water like an out-of-control ice skater.

Its jerky, spastic dance was worse than any horror movie, because this was *real*. A tremor wracked my body, and I curled my arms protectively around my midsection.

I knew what I was seeing, and I didn't *want* to see it but couldn't look away. A hysterical laugh burbled up in my throat.

And though I'd never been at a death scene before, I was fairly certain laughing would be considered strange and inappropriate. I slapped my hands to my face and choked the horror back, but an odd sound slipped out.

"What did you say?" Denton cocked his head, his blue eyes narrowing.

The ghost staggered and fell to his knees. Its head ducked beneath the water. Its body jerked.

Shaking my head, I squeezed my hands tighter. *Act normal. Act normal.* "Nothing," I croaked.

Abe's motions grew more erratic. His loafers kicked. The deputy's expression shifted from concern to wariness.

Weird Lenore. That's what the kids had called me. The whole town thought I was weird, though some were better at hiding it than others.

"It's... just... shocking," I stammered. *Weird Lenore.* "Finding someone."

The movement of the ghost's limbs slowed. Water darkened his jeans and green jacket, spreading like a stain.

"You did good." Denton moved slowly, cautiously, toward me. Awkwardly, he patted my shoulder. "Holding it together, I mean, calling us. I know it was rough finding him."

The body collapsed and went limp. The back of the ghost's head emerged from the swimming hole and bobbed, face down. Darkness oozed from a wound in the back of its scalp.

"Th—thanks," I said.

Because I couldn't think of anything else to say, I fled. By the time I'd returned to my Volvo, I'd calmed down enough to realize what I'd seen—the ghost's murder.

Abe hadn't simply slipped, banged his head, and drowned. He'd fought someone—someone who'd shoved his head beneath the water and held it there.

But that wound at the back of his head... He'd been hit with something first. It hadn't been quite enough to render him unconscious, but it might have weakened him, rendering him more vulnerable.

I stared at my hands on the wheel. The police were investigating. So what if Sheriff McCourt was out of town? She'd return eventually, or the county would assign someone else to manage the case.

I looked up. The redheaded deputy stood beside Abe's flower-power van and studied me.

They'll figure out it's murder on their own. I pulled from the lot, drove down the tree-lined highway, and took the turn into Doyle. *The police have got this.* I crossed the humpbacked stone bridge into town, and my shoulders loosened.

My car coasted past summer tourists wandering raised wooden sidewalks. As a kid, I'd thought my hometown—a 19th century mining town—was boring. "Downtown" consisted of only one street, and it wasn't very long.

But a part of me had always loved its old-west false fronts, its stone buildings, its gardens penned behind wrought-iron fences. Ghosts seemed almost *normal* walking its historic streets, where the layers of time were more obvious.

Doyle was a wine town now, its old stone barns and wooden shops converted to tasting rooms. The forests and dormant volcano drew hikers. We even had a few UFO tourists, which a solitary B&B catered to.

On auto pilot, I turned off Main Street and drove down residential roads, past Victorians and cabins separated by wide yards, and pulled into our driveway. I turned off the ignition and sat, the Volvo ticking as it cooled.

I'd grown up in this fairytale house of peaked roofs, arched windows, and black doors. Aunt Ellen had gotten the idea for the painted doors, she'd said, from a visit to London in her younger years. I'd loved all three stories of memories and magic.

I exhaled slowly and stepped from the car, my shoes crunching on the gravel drive. Grabbing my pack from the seat beside me, I shut the car door and moved toward the house.

I climbed the porch steps, letting my fingers trail along the wooden railing to ground me. Ellen sat in the porch rocker, a mug of tea steaming on the nearby wicker table.

My aunt matched her house, her button up shirt and slacks as neat as its shingle and stone sides. Ellen's pixie-cut brown hair might be graying at the temples, but not a wisp of hair or branch in the yard dared be out of place.

"How's the job hunt—?" Her blue eyes narrowed. She leaned forward. "What's happened? Your aura..."

"I was hiking," I said shortly. Having a guardian who could supernaturally sus out your emotions had been irritating when I was a child. It still made me feel vulnerable. "I found a body in Doyle Creek."

Ellen sucked in a breath. "Did you call the police?"

"Of course," I said heavily. "I waited and showed them where I'd found him."

"Oh, no. The look on your face... Was there a ghost?"

"Yes." I rubbed my cheek and studied the porch's wooden planks. If Abe had died within the last twenty-four hours, it was unusually quick for his ghost to manifest. Unusual, but not impossible.

"Did the ghost speak to you?"

"No," I said, neck stiffening. This was so typical of Ellen. I'd found a body—not typical—and all she cared about was whether I'd had an opportunity to practice my mediumship.

A part of me wondered if she was so obsessed with my magic because magic came so hard to her. The other part of me slapped that thought down hard. Ellen could be irritating, but she loved us. She'd demonstrated that love daily.

"It will speak," she said. "If the ghost came to you, it will come again."

"Why?" I burst out. "Why me? Jayce has nice, normal earth magic, and Karin doesn't have any magic—"

"Don't be so sure of that."

"My sisters don't see dead people, and I don't want to."

Ghosts were terrifying and needy, and I couldn't help them. If I could send them off into the light, that would be one thing. But to watch them torment themselves and not be able to help...

"Keep talking to them," Ellen said in a low voice. "They have stories to tell, and your gift is your power and your protection."

"Protection from what?" I glanced at the broom leaning beside the shiny black front door. Ellen insisted on keeping one there for magical protection. But aside from the potential forest fire, what was there to fear in small-town Doyle?

"There are dangerous things in this world and the others. You know this. You've *seen* what's there."

I didn't *want* to see it. But complaining wouldn't change anything.

Clamping my mouth shut, I forced down my irritation. It wasn't Ellen I was annoyed with—it was the situation I couldn't change. I wished my sisters were here, instead of at a theater festival in Sonoma.

"It was a hiker, I suppose," Ellen mused. "People don't take nature seriously."

"What?"

"The dead person. Was it a hiker? Your ghost must have unfinished business. Wouldn't you like to be able to help?"

"No. I mean, yes, of course I want to help. It just never works out that way. And he must have been hiking, but he wasn't a tourist. It was Abe Crowe."

Ellen stilled on the porch rocker. "I see. How awful." She picked her mug off the wicker table and took a sip.

A crow cawed in the front yard. Its presence struck me as ironic rather than ominous though.

"Well," she said. "You're still young, and things will happen in your own time." She shook her head. "It's wrong of me to push you. If you don't want to talk to his ghost, don't talk to it."

Ah... what? Ellen had never backed off getting me to embrace my "gift" before. *Why now?* "I think he was murdered."

"You said he didn't say anything to you," her voice razored.

"He didn't. He... acted it out."

"Good lord." Ellen touched her throat, where a silver Celtic knot charm lay. "No wonder you're still upset." She reached across the low wicker table and grasped my hand. "I'm sorry you had to see that."

"I didn't tell the police." My voice broke. "I didn't know how or what—"

"Of course not. Don't worry about it. I'll take care of it."

I shifted the backpack on my shoulder. "How?" Ellen might be friends with Sherriff McCourt, but I knew they didn't talk magic. Our magic was kept private, secret.

"Never mind that. Any luck with the job hunt?" Ellen asked cheerfully. "I saw there was a new help-wanted sign in the bookstore window today."

My mouth flattened. Oh, she was definitely changing the subject. "How well did you know Abe Crowe?" I probed.

"Not well. I do, however, know Mike at the bookstore fairly well. Would you like me to talk to him?"

I pulled the rune sticker from the rear pocket of my khakis. "These were floating in the creek where I found Abe. Do you recognize this rune?"

My aunt glanced at it. "That's not a rune."

"It looks like one."

"Well, it's not." Ellen rose, cradling the mug to her chest. The rocker swayed, bouncing off the backs of her calves. The crow fluttered from an oak tree and landed beside a lavender bush.

I shook my head. "The sticker might be connected to Abe—"

"And as you said, the police were there."

"But—"

"If Abe got himself into trouble," she said sharply, "that's his business, not ours." She yanked open the black front door and strode into the house.

Ellen was hiding something.

My aunt was hiding something, and it hadn't been the first time she'd kept things from me. Heat rose in my chest. This time, I wasn't going to let it go.

Chapter 4

PUSHING ELLEN NEVER WORKED. My jaw set.

I decided to push her anyway.

I walked inside the house, automatically wiping my feet on the blue rag rug by the door. Ellen strode into the kitchen, and I followed.

She stood on the other side of the butcher block island, her slim back to me. The drying herbs hanging above the island partially hid her movements.

Ellen took a teapot from a moss-green cupboard. She turned, clutching it to her chest.

"You know something." I set my backpack on the counter. "You're hiding something."

Ellen blanched and took a step backward, bumping against the butcher block counter. "No." Her gaze shifted toward a glass bottle on the counter by the old-fashioned gas stove.

I strode to the counter and picked up the spray bottle filled with her vinegar and water cleaning solution. A rune drawn in Ellen's careful script adorned one side. "This rune is for protection," I said.

Ellen's knuckles whitened on the teapot. The wall clock ticked.

"What's the rune on the sticker for?" I asked.

Her shoulders relaxed. "I told you," she said coldly, "it's not a rune—or at least not like any rune I've ever seen."

"But you recognized it," I guessed.

Ellen set the teapot on the island and left the kitchen. When she returned, she held a thick paperback in one hand. "Take a look." She opened it to a page lined with columns of runes.

I scanned the page. There was no rune like the one on the sticker. But... My pulse quickened. "It looks like a combination of two runes mashed together—Ansuz and Eiwaz."

I read aloud. "*Eiwaz is used in runic magic for protection, spiritual insight, and connecting with ancestral or cosmic wisdom. Ansuz represents divine inspiration, insight, and altered states of consciousness.*"

Ellen leaned against the counter. "I'm glad you're finally getting more interested in divination. But is it so hard to understand that I don't want you mixed up in a murder?" she asked more gently.

I set the paperback on the butcher block island. "But—"

"If I knew anything, I would tell the sheriff. And if Abe's ghost comes to you again, you don't owe him anything. He has no more right to mix you up in his business now that he's dead than he did when he was alive."

"But what *was* his business?" I asked.

"He didn't have any. Abe was retired. He used to be an environmental engineer, and lately his hobby has been environmental activism. I'm pretty sure that's why his wife left him," she added dryly.

His wife had been the best dressed woman in Doyle and constantly complained about how small the town was. When she'd left for Florida, more than a few people had been relieved.

I scraped my teeth across my bottom lip. Now was the time for me to drop it. The murder had nothing to do with us, and I didn't want to play ghost whisperer. But I dug in. "Could he have been killed over this activism?"

"That is an obvious line of inquiry which I'm sure the sheriff will pursue." She moved to a cupboard. Opening it, she pulled out a slender tea tin.

"Sheriff McCourt's not here," I said. "That... trouble over her husband."

Ellen's mouth puckered. She filled a strainer with loose tea. "Poor woman. She's up for election next year. This can't help her chances."

A few dried leaves fell upon the butcherblock counter. Ellen swiped them up with the edge of her hand and dropped them into her mug. "Now, when do you think you'll finish that bookcase?"

It was another subject change, and I couldn't get anything more out of my aunt about Abe after that. I managed not to slam any doors in frustration. Barely.

I saw Abe in my dreams that night. He'd come, as Ellen had predicted. He didn't say anything. He'd just repeated that murderous pantomime.

My aunt didn't ask me about him the next morning though. When I mentioned his name, there seemed something almost fearful in her terse response. She didn't warn me Crowe's ghost would keep coming until he was satisfied.

She didn't have to. I knew it was true.

There was nothing noble about my motivations as I strode past the restaurants and tasting rooms on Main Street, heat dampening my light-weight white blouse. Back then, I still let my emotions guide me.

There was only one way to keep Abe out of my dreams, but that wasn't entirely why I decided to dig deeper into his death. I was irritated with Ellen. If I dug deeper, I was annoyed with myself, too.

I pushed through the batwing doors of Antoine's bar. They swung shut behind me on creaky hinges. Light from the old-timey brass lamps overhead dimly illuminated the room. On the far wall, the jukebox sat dark and silent.

It was the end of the weekend and tourist season. Half the round tables on the sawdust floor were full. So were the booths along the long wall.

I walked to the antique bar. Antoine polished a beer mug behind it with a white dishcloth. He was a big man, with a thick waist bound by his apron. Curly gray hair lay tight against his head.

The bar owner glanced up at me. "Hi, Lenore," he rumbled. "You here for a late lunch?"

I smiled. Antoine had always been kind to me, even though, unlike my sisters, I wasn't much of a bar person.

On our twenty-first birthday, my sisters and I had come to Antoine's. I'd gotten violently, embarrassingly ill. Antoine had told me that's what sawdust was for, advised drinking lots of water, and called a taxi.

The next time I'd seen him, my face burning with humiliation, he'd simply smiled and asked how my day was going and moved on. I'd never gone too far with alcohol again, and I considered Antoine a friend.

I knew I wasn't special though. Antoine was everyone's friend. Even non-drinkers came to Antoine's bar. If anyone knew the gossip on Abe Crowe, it would be Antoine.

I hiked myself onto one of the crimson bar stools. "I already ate. May I have a club soda?"

Antoine angled his graying head and smiled. "Why not?" Moving down the counter, he filled the mug from a soda gun and handed it to me.

"Did you hear about Abe Crowe?" I asked in a low voice and winced. I sounded like a cheap gossip. "I found his body yesterday morning when I was hiking up by Doyle Creek."

Antoine stilled, then braced his hands on the bar, his round shoulders hunching. "I heard. He was here Thursday, and—" He shook his head. "I'm sorry for Abe, but I'm sorrier for you."

"Why for me?"

He grimaced. "Finding his body couldn't have been easy on you. As for Abe... He knew how to get under people's skins. He enjoyed it."

It *hadn't* been easy, and I swallowed. "Whose skin did he get under?"

A diner raised a hand, catching Antoine's attention. The bar owner nodded to a couple at one of the round tables. "Excuse me." He ambled around the bar, pulling a notepad from the pocket of his apron.

They spoke briefly. Antoine tore a receipt from the pad and set it on the table then returned to the bar.

"You said Abe was in the bar Thursday?" I sipped my mug of club soda.

"Yeah." He picked up a glass mug and polished it with his towel. "He left around four. Said he wanted to get a hike in before it got dark. Why?"

So Abe hadn't been planning a night hike. It was June, the solstice was coming, and darkness fell close to nine o'clock. "The rain started around eight that night," I muttered. "Abe must have arrived at the trailhead before then."

Antoine's coffee eyes softened. "It's natural to try to figure out what happened when someone dies suddenly. But I wouldn't worry about Abe. If he's dead, he's past worrying about."

Abe didn't have children to mourn him. Would his ex-wife? Did she even know he was dead? "Did he have many friends?"

The bar owner shook his head. "He was a bona fide pain in the... butt."

"What do you mean?" I asked. The jukebox started up—a John Denver song.

"You know Caleb Morse's lumber operation?" Antoine jerked his head toward the batwing doors. A motorcycle grumbled past outside.

I knew where the lumber mill was, and I nodded.

"Abe was giving him trouble about it."

"Trouble?"

"Accused him of over harvesting trees. With the fire danger so high, I figure Caleb can cut as many trees as he wants. He always plants new ones. But Abe..." He shrugged his rounded shoulders. "You know how fanatics can be."

I didn't know. Not then. But I agreed with Antoine anyway. "Thanks." Finishing my soda, I left some bills on the bar and returned to my Volvo.

I sat behind the wheel, debating my next move. My enthusiasm for amateur detecting was ebbing. Abe's death wasn't my business. And Ellen was right; I didn't owe the man anything—dead or alive.

But Ellen had been hiding something, and that bothered me.

Also, I really did need to finish that bookcase.

"The hell with it." I started the car.

I drove up the mountain toward Caleb's logging operation, turning off the highway onto a roughly paved road. After a quarter mile, the pavement turned to dirt. The road narrowed, pines and a steep drop hemming in my car.

Growing up in the Sierras, I was used to mountain driving. But after the third lumber truck passed, forcing me close to the road's edge, I was sweating.

Finally, I rounded a bend, and the road opened up to a dirt lot. My hands unclenched on the wheel. Behind a wire-mesh fence, a massive mechanical claw shifted piles of uncut logs.

The whine of a motorized saw pierced the air and echoed off the valley walls. A warm breeze surged through the pines, and they bent in response.

I parked far from the low wooden sales building to give myself more time to think. Palms damp on the steering wheel, I sat in my car.

On the drive, I'd thought up and rejected half a dozen conversational gambits. I still had no idea how to approach Caleb. Asking to buy a cut two-by-four seemed an easy start though.

I didn't get out of the car.

My aunt's voice echoed in my ears. *If you got out more, you'd get over your shyness. All you need is practice.*

I grimaced, staring at the small wooden building where lumber was sold to the locals. My sisters wouldn't have hesitated. Jayce would just say whatever came into her head. Karin, a writer, always seemed to know the right thing to say.

I hunched deeper in my seat. This was silly. The lumber company was a business. They had to talk to a customer. *Right?*

Insides jittering, I stepped from the car. I walked toward the building with its *Lumber for Sale* sign above the yellow door.

As I reached the open door, the mechanical saw fell silent. I stopped short, hovering in the doorway. Inside, two men squared off in front of a long, wooden counter.

"How long do you think you can keep this up?" a thick-set, middle-aged man asked. His arm was in a sling over his blue dress shirt, the boots beneath his khakis coated with mud. I recognized him a local, Wharton Van Goethe.

"You're going under." Wharton raked a hand through his brown hair specked with gray. "You can sell now and walk away clean, or you can sell to me later when the price is lower."

I gnawed the inside of my cheek. Jonas had asked about Wharton, and now Wharton was here. *Coincidence?*

But that was the problem with small towns—it *could* be coincidence. When everyone was connected somehow, it was easy to see relationships that weren't there.

Behind the counter, Caleb Morse grimaced. "I don't need you to tell me my business." He was a hulking man, over six feet tall and with thinning, sandy blond hair, like a balding grizzly. The sleeves of his plaid green shirt were edged with mud.

Was the lumber company in trouble? Maybe Abe had had more of a financial impact on Caleb than Antoine had thought. I made myself small and hoped they wouldn't notice me. The saw started up again, and I jumped a little.

Caleb looked toward me, wavering in the doorway, and he blinked. "You looking for lumber?"

A wooden fox the size of my thumb sat on the counter beside a pocketknife. Caleb whittled the tiny animals and left them on mailboxes and benches. People collected them as good luck charms. I even had one of his miniature deer on my bureau.

"Ah..." *Say something. Be cool. Subtle.* But panicked, I'd forgotten my bookcase excuse. I rubbed my palms on the front of my pale slacks.

Caleb exhaled slowly and smiled. "Cat got your tongue?" He picked up the knife and a small block of wood.

Say something. "It's about Abe Crowe," I blurted. "He's dead." I cringed. *Not subtle. Not subtle at all.*

"I heard." Caleb's knife dug into the wood. "Tragic," he said insincerely.

Wharton cocked his head, lips pursed. "Dead?" He adjusted the sling and winced. "I hadn't heard that."

"It happened yesterday," I said. "I mean, the body was found yesterday. In Doyle Creek."

Caleb stopped whittling. "You haven't become one of his environmental kids?" His neck corded, color rising to his fleshy cheeks. "I'm not over harvesting. I've never over harvested. And I don't need you putting my men in more danger. Spikes can make a chainsaw kick back, or a blade shatter, or a chain whip."

Spikes? I took a step backward, my shoulders crumpling inward defensively. "I'm not— I need a two-by-four."

"Abe Crowe is dead?" Wharton repeated as if I hadn't spoken. His head turned. He studied Caleb. "That's... convenient."

The two stared at each other silently. Caleb set down the knife and wood and folded his arms.

Ask a question. Do something. "Convenient?" I squeaked.

"But it won't save your business." Wharton raised a dark eyebrow. "How many of your men quit after what he did to that grove?"

"What—what grove?" Heat flushed my body.

"Someone spiked Caleb's trees near a spring east of here," Wharton said.

Oh, tree spiking. It *was* horribly dangerous for loggers.

"Not someone—those pot growers." Caleb clawed a hand through his sandy hair. "They want my men to stay clear of their grove, even if it is on my property."

"Or environmentalists did it," Wharton said helpfully. "The problem is, if they spiked one grove, they may have spiked others. It's spooked folks."

Caleb's fleshy face darkened. "It's just the one grove. And if I had evidence Abe spiked those trees, I would have gone to the cops."

"Would you have though?" Wharton said thoughtfully. "I saw you in Antoine's Thursday evening. You weren't talking about cops then."

Then what *had* Caleb been talking about that night? "Did you... see Abe at Antoine's?" I asked, fumbling my way forward.

"What?" Caleb retrieved the knife and chunk of wood.

"Abe was at Antoine's Thursday," I said. "He was there until around four."

"No." Caleb peeled a long strip off the wood. "I was there later, at eight."

"And before then?" I asked. My face warmed. Now I was asking about alibis? I was *horrible* at talking to people, much less interrogating them. I *did* need more practice.

Caleb's face reddened. "What are you saying? That he was murdered? Are you asking for my alibi?"

I stammered. "No, no. That wasn't—"

"Now, I'm curious too," Wharton said to Caleb. "What *were* you doing before eight?"

"I wanted that fool, Abe, arrested," Caleb said. "It was Mira who wanted him dead, and if the cops come asking, that's what I'll tell 'em."

My heart dropped. *Mira?*

That... might explain what my aunt had been hiding.

Chapter 5

ANOTHER PROBLEM WITH SMALL towns is TMI—too much information. There are things I don't *want* to know. If X is having an affair with Y, if Z has a gambling problem... Sometimes, it's easier to like people when you know less about them.

And I liked Ellen's friend, Mira. I didn't want to hear she wanted someone dead. Mira was like Antoine—kind. I didn't want to believe there was more to her than that, that she might be a real person with flaws and secret shames.

But I swallowed hard and blundered onward anyway. "Mira?"

Neither of the men responded. Outside, the mechanical saw shrieked. A breeze through the open door carried the scent of sawdust.

Caleb shifted, glowering behind the counter and kept whittling. A rough, feline head emerged from the block of wood.

"Mira Tate?" I pressed. "The herbalist? What does she have to do with Abe Crowe?"

Mira owned a small shop in an alley off Main Street. "Small" was actually understating the case. It was only as wide as a walk-in closet, and not one of those big walk-ins you see in the home improvement shows.

The fact that her herbal store was next to a spice shop hadn't deterred her one bit. "I don't sell cooking herbs," she always said with a smile.

"You should ask her yourself," Caleb said in a more even tone. His bushy brows tugged downward. "Are you here for gossip or for lumber?"

My toes curled. *Forget the bookcase.* "Sorry. I'm leaving," I muttered and hurried into the parking lot.

A murder of crows, their caws echoing across the hardpacked lot, perched on a red pickup. I speedwalked toward my Volvo. So, that had been a disaster. I hadn't even gotten my two-by-four, and there was no way I was going back for it now.

I couldn't ask Mira about Abe. Ellen would be furious. Mira might be insulted.

And those were all excuses. I didn't want to shatter my image of the sweet herbalist. But should I warn her of Caleb's threat?

The air whispered around my ears. Wings beat the air. Something hit the back of my head, and I jerked forward. A crow flew away, shrieking. The bird dropped onto the pickup, displacing other black birds.

I hurried toward my car and touched my head where the crow had struck. The bird hadn't drawn blood. Irrationally embarrassed, I glanced around the lot to see if anyone had noticed the attack.

Two of the crows leapt from the truck and zoomed toward me, low and fast. I shrieked and ducked, hands protecting my head. Talons scraped the back of my hand.

Keeping low, I hurried toward my Volvo. My hands shook. Why had I parked so far from the sales building? The crows circled for another attack. I broke into a frantic run, visions of Hitchcock movies in my head.

A red-tailed hawk sped between the birds. The two crows scattered, tumbling in the air. The hawk screamed, and the other crows exploded off the truck. The hawk soared above the pines, the crows giving chase.

Hands trembling, I got into my car and checked my hand. No skin was broken, but my pride was in tatters. I slammed the door shut.

— *ele* —

I knew Mira's herbal shop well. My aunt had taken us there often enough for sage and other herbs.

Mira and my aunt had been friends since forever, they said. Was that why Ellen had clammed up when she'd learned of Abe's death? Was she covering for Mira? I wasn't sure, and I hated my uncertainty.

Mira had been kind to me, letting me linger in her shop when childhood bullies had been on the street. *You're not weird, you're an introvert. That's its own superpower.*

I opened the wooden door and hesitated, peering inside the long, narrow space. Shelves filled with brown-glass jars of herbs lined the walls. A sunbeam from the round skylight streamed through the drying herbs hanging from the rafters.

Mira sat on a high wooden stool behind a tall, square worktable at the back of the room. Squinting, she shielded her eyes with one hand. "Lenore? Is that you? I can't see much with the backlighting."

A wiry woman in her late forties, Mira's gray-streaked ebony hair was pulled into a tight bun, accentuating sharp cheekbones and sunken green eyes. She wiped her roughened hands on the crisp apron over her faded cotton dress.

I stepped from the doorway. "Good guess."

Mira smiled. "Not really. Your aunt said you'd be by."

I started. How had Ellen known? I hadn't told her I was planning on coming here. I hadn't known myself until about thirty minutes ago.

"I have the palo santo she needed." Rising, she squeezed around the workbench and walked to a closed blue cupboard. Opening its doors, she pulled out a paper bag and handed it to me.

"Thanks." Bemused, I opened the bag and inhaled. The scent of palo santo beat that of burning sage, hands down.

"Ellen's already paid," Mira said.

"Oh. Okay." I clutched the bag to my chest and didn't move. "What are you working on?"

"A healing salve for Wharton Van Goethe. He hurt his shoulder quite badly last Tuesday." She tsked. "I've never seen a shoulder so purple that wasn't dislocated. The poor man has barely been able to move it."

"Mm." If Mira told Ellen I'd asked her about Abe... But Ellen was already annoyed with me. It was Mira I didn't want to offend. Maybe I should drop it.

"Was there something else you wanted?" she asked gently.

I cleared my throat. But instead of telling her I'd been the one to find Abe's body and Caleb just might rat her out to the cops, I pulled the sticker from my pocket. "Do you recognize this rune?"

Her face tightened. "Where did you find that?"

"Abe Cr—"

"Abe," she spat. "Even in death, that man's causing trouble."

"Ellen said Abe—"

"You should listen to your aunt. She had the measure of the man."

"She doesn't seem to—didn't seem to like him much. I—"

"Why would she like him?" Mira laughed, a hard, short, cutting sound. "What he was doing up at that spring is blasphemy. He—" The herbalist's expression shifted. Mira's face turned ashen. Tendons bulged in her neck.

The air stilled, dust motes hanging motionless in a sunbeam. A cloud passed over the late afternoon sun, and the cramped shop darkened.

"Mira?" I asked. The shadows of the herbs hanging from the rafters grew long, stretching, covering Mira's face in dark splotches.

And then I felt it. Cold. Not a natural cold, not the cold of a confused spirit. This cold had a presence, cruel and cunning. It pressed against me, squeezing my lungs, slicking my skin, pebbling my flesh.

I was afraid. I'd never felt fear in Mira's shop before, but now it trembled up my spine, gripped my heart in cold, skeletal fingers.

And Mira felt it too. She stood frozen, lips parted, eyes staring helpless and hollow. I wanted to reach for her, to grasp her calloused hand, but my arms were locked at my sides.

The door flung open, banging against the back wall, and Mira and I yelped. A tall, broad figure loomed, silhouetted in the doorway by the blinding sunlight.

Mira shrank back. "No," she whispered. "I didn't tell. I didn't tell."

The figure stepped inside. It resolved to a man in an expensive suit—tall, broad shouldered, thirtyish with slicked back brown hair. I gulped a breath like someone coming up for air from the bottom of a Sierra lake.

The man moved past me, forcing me to press against one wall to make way. His muscled form seemed to take up more space in that small shop than it should have, like a magic box larger on the inside than the outside but inverted.

"Mira Tate?" he rumbled.

"That's, ah, me." The older woman cleared her throat, the color returning to her cheeks. "That's— How can I help you?"

"I'm Detective Vanning, from Sacramento." He pulled a wallet from the inside pocket of his blazer and showed a badge. "I need to ask you some questions about Abe Crowe."

Mira studied the badge. Her sun spotted hands trembled. "Why?"

"Because I understood you knew the man, and he's dead." He glanced down at me. His eyes were iced coffee. "Who are you?"

"Lenore Bonheim." Hastily, I pocketed the rune sticker. What had just happened? I'd never experienced anything like it. Had I imagined that supernatural cold and Mira's strange transformation?

I *must* have imagined it. The pungent herbs, the dim lighting, my sharp-edged nerves had all combined to trick me into seeing malice in the air.

"The girl who found the body." The detective nodded. "You can go."

Swallowing, I edged from the herbal shop. They'd brought in a detective from Sacramento. The police must think Abe's death wasn't accidental. I didn't have to pursue this. The cops had it handled.

The shop door drifted shut slowly behind me. Slowly enough for me to linger outside and listen, and I paused beside the wooden wall, partly because I still couldn't quite believe what had happened.

And partly because I want to hear what Mira would say.

"What can you tell me about Abe Crowe?" the detective asked.

"He's—he was a local environmentalist."

"I heard you were shouting at him in the street Thursday morning," he said. "What was that about?"

"Who told you that?"

The door's edge rested against the red-painted molding. Back to the wall, I pressed my fingertips to the door, keeping it open just enough to hear. But the detective didn't respond.

"I was damned sick and tired of him bringing in all the potheads," Mira finally said. "They'd end up at my shop, looking for weed, and when I didn't have any, they'd stick around, cluttering the place up, and driving off my paying customers."

"Potheads?"

"He's got an illegal grove up in the mountains. If the cops had bothered to do something about that when I'd complained earlier, maybe Abe wouldn't be dead."

Illegal grove? Abe was responsible for the marijuana Wharton and Caleb had mentioned?

The detective grunted. "Where were you between five and eight PM Thursday night?"

"Here, in my shop."

"Did anyone see you?"

"No."

"The sign on your door says your shop closes at six," Detective Vanning said.

Chest squeezing, I pressed tighter against the rough wood wall. But if they'd looked toward the door when he'd mention the sign in its window, they seemed not to have noticed it hadn't quite closed.

"It does," Mira said, "and sometimes I stay later than that to work. I don't know why you're bothering me. Shouldn't you be looking into who benefits from Abe's death?"

"And who do you think benefits?"

"That dirt bag who's been helping Abe sell his weed. He'll probably take over the operation now."

The door slipped against my damp fingertips. Grimacing, I pressed harder.

The sun was hot, the alley without any shade beyond that from the low wooden buildings. It heated the bricks beneath my feet and scalded my skin.

The detective coughed. "The dirt bag being..."

"His name is Jonas," the herbalist said. "He's not from here. I don't know him, and I don't know his last name."

"Right. Small town insularity. The outsider is always guilty, because it's easier not to believe any of you lot could have done it."

"There's nothing wrong with small towns," Mira said stiffly.

"If you say so."

"I *do* say so. We're quiet. We help each other. There's hardly any crime..." she trailed off.

Vanning huffed a laugh.

A tourist in a loose tank top and board shorts ambled past and shot me a curious look. I flushed.

"Jonas and Abe were involved in drug dealing." Mira's voice was firm. "Look into that."

"I have," he said. "They're small time."

"Their production may have been small, but they got a premium for their marijuana."

"Why?"

Mira muttered something indistinct. "...Jonas."

"We'll talk to Jonas when we find him," the detective said. "Right now, I want your alibi."

"I had no reason to kill Abe."

"According to three witnesses, you wished him dead."

"That was..." She sputtered. "I was angry, that was all."

"Angry enough to kill?"

The door slipped off my fingertips, and I sucked in a quick breath. It closed with a loud snick.

Chapter 6

I DARTED AROUND THE corner of the building before Mira or the detective could investigate the noise. Face hot, I hurried down the alley. I glanced over my shoulder. The alley was empty.

When had I ever eavesdropped before? This wasn't like me.

I didn't tell. That wasn't like Mira either. She'd looked terrified before she'd realized the figure in the doorway had been a detective.

I stopped short beside the door to the spice shop that Mira claimed wasn't a competitor. The scent of cinnamon and cloves hung in the air.

I don't think I'd ever heard her use the word "blasphemy" before either. It was as if for a moment she hadn't been Mira, as if someone else had been looking through her eyes.

And *what* hadn't she told? Because she'd thought someone who wasn't the detective had been in that doorway, and it had scared her. Badly. Who had she thought had been standing there?

Or what?

Ridiculous. I shook myself. *Whats* might float through my vision on occasion, but they weren't a part of Mira's world, and Mira had been scared of that figure in the doorway.

A schoolgirl nemesis, Mary Hannon, stepped from the spice shop. Even in her black spice shop apron, she looked poised and lovely. A smear of orange—turmeric, I guessed—brightened the apron's front pocket.

Mary flicked a wary glance in my direction. One corner of her mouth curled in derision. "What are *you* doing here, Lenore?"

"Just... walking."

"Huh." She tossed her long, glossy brown hair and strode away.

My hands fisted. In the fifth grade, Mary had bullied me whenever she'd gotten the chance. But we weren't fifth graders anymore. I jammed my hands into my loose pockets and continued to Main Street.

It was late afternoon, and more tourists wandered Doyle's raised, wood-plank sidewalks. A hotel worker high on a ladder hung American flag bunting on the white-painted balconies of the pale blue hotel across the street. Its wrought iron shutters were shut against the heat.

I crossed the road and walked away from the action, deeper into Main Street's canopy of elms. Automatically, I headed for the bookstore—my favorite place to shop.

At its door, I stopped short. A *Help Wanted* sign hung in its window.

Ellen had been right again. And I loved books. A bookstore should be the ideal job for me. Except I didn't love spending time with people, and the job was customer service.

Movement across the street caught my attention. An elm branch sagged violently. A massive red-tailed hawk studied me from the swaying branch.

I crossed the narrow road and looked up beside a wrought-iron bench. "Thanks for helping with those crows."

Stomach fluttering, I looked around. How could I blame people for thinking I was *weird Lenore* if I talked to birds? Fortunately, most people were at the other end of the street, by the t-shirt shops and restaurants and tasting rooms.

"You're probably not even the same hawk," I muttered, feeling even more foolish. But no one was around to hear me, and it wasn't as if the bird could understand.

"You are welcome, Shaman," a masculine voice said, strong and clear.

"What?" My head whipped around.

I was alone. But the voice had sounded close, almost like it was... on top... of me.

I glanced toward the hotel worker on the ladder a block away. No. *Too far.* It hadn't been his voice I'd heard. I looked up into the tree.

The hawk stared down, its golden eyes impassive.

"Did you... say something?" I asked.

The bird didn't respond.

"Right." I licked my lips, the hairs lifting on the back of my neck. "I'm going crazy, that's all." And maybe I should shut up before anyone noticed.

"Most shamans are perceived that way."

I froze, heart leaping into my throat. It had been the hawk. It *must* have been the hawk. But I didn't talk to birds, only to...

I gripped the back of the bench beside me. "Are you dead?" But that didn't make sense either. The animal ghosts I'd encountered never talked to me.

The bird launched himself from the branch. I flung up my arm. A line of fire raked my flesh, and I cried out, ducking.

The bird vanished.

I straightened, clutching my forearm, scanning the false fronts, the rooftops, the trees for another attack. But the hawk had disappeared.

Three slashes marked my arm, oozing blood. What had he done *that* for? And I'd been feeling so pleased when the crow hadn't drawn blood. Muttering a curse, I hurried toward my car, parked several blocks away on Main.

As I passed the bookstore, a shape emerged from the alley on its other side. I glanced over my shoulder.

Jonas strolled behind me, a wooden matchstick between his teeth. He shrugged his shoulders beneath his denim jacket and didn't meet my gaze.

My sister Jayce would seize the moment, turn around and talk to him. But I was bleeding, and my arm hurt, and I wasn't my sister. I crossed the street toward Antoine's.

Jonas did too. I rubbed my damp palms on the front of my slacks.

He probably wasn't following me. Lots of locals went to Antoine's. Why *would* Jonas follow me? Because he'd seen me in the trailhead parking lot?

I walked through the bar's old-west bat wing doors. Jonas boots clomped on the raised wooden sidewalk behind me and kept going.

I hurried to the ladies room and cleaned up. Plastering a paper towel to my forearm as a bandage, I rolled down the sleeve of my white blouse to cover it. Then I got a booth and ordered a cheeseburger.

I discovered I was hungry and ate the burger quickly, not really tasting it. After I paid, I emerged from the bar and walked down the block.

Boots clunked on the sidewalk behind me. I sped up and glanced over my shoulder. *Jonas.* My heart jumped. I continued another block then crossed the street again.

Jonas did too. My insides quivered, and I blinked rapidly, stomach churning. Jonas really was following me.

A couple sat on an iron bench in the little parklike area surrounding the thatched, circular stone hut that was the Doyle Visitors' Center.

I hurried through the small building's yellow door. The stone room was blessedly cool. Brochure racks lined its curved walls.

A smiling, gray-haired woman looked up from her desk. "Lenore? What can I do for you?" She adjusted her cat-eye glasses, attached to a chain around her neck. "Oh, my goodness. What happened to your arm?"

A miner with a tangled gray beard and saggy jeans braced his hands on his desk and howled into her face. "Git outta my house!"

"Oh, hi Mrs. Templeton," I said, ignoring the ghost. I'd seen it before—it was one of the first ghosts I'd tried to help. *Unsuccessfully.*

I glanced down at my arm. Blood had seeped through the sleeve of my blouse. "I didn't know you'd be working today, and it's just a scratch."

"I'm here most Saturdays," she said placidly, opening a desk drawer and pulling out a first aid kit. "What brings you to the Visitors' Center?" She opened the kit, pulled out a squirt bottle of alcohol, and handed it to me.

"Thanks." Rolling up my sleeve, I peeled off the paper towel then ran the alcohol over my cuts. Before the liquid could drip to the stone floor, she passed me white cheesecloth bandages. I blotted my arm, then wrapped it hastily.

"You should rinse that blouse in cold water," Mrs. Templeton said.

The miner kicked the desk, his leg going through its wooden panel. "Out!"

"I was, ah..." My brain scrambled for something sensible to say. "I wanted to ask about springs around Doyle," I said, thinking of the spring Caleb had mentioned.

"Oh." She folded her hands on the desk, her mouth pinching. "We don't usually give that information out."

"Why not?" I asked, surprised.

"Because we don't want anyone trying to find them. Do you have any idea how many people get lost in the mountains?"

I did. People vanished into the Sierra woods on a regular basis. Many were never found again.

"Oh," I said, unaccountably disappointed, since the spring had only been an excuse. But I *was* curious about the spring where Abe had spiked Caleb's trees.

"Dammit, woman. This ain't your house."

Mrs. Templeton leaned forward, a conspiratorial look on her round face. "One's not such a secret. I'm sure you know the spring the teens all go to..."

She trailed off, her plump cheeks reddening, probably remembering I'd been home schooled. Mrs. Templeton cleared her throat. "And then there's the spring that's the source of Doyle Creek. Snow melt feeds into it too, of course. That's on private property though."

"Caleb Morse's?"

"Yes." Her gaze slid to a carved wooden rabbit on the corner of her desk. "It's posted no trespassing, which is another reason we don't give that information out. Also, I don't know exactly where it is."

Her fleshy stomach pressed deeper against the desk. "The fairies don't like it when people go there." She pressed a finger to her lips then laughed.

I did also, too long and too loud, trying not to look at the ghost.

"Shut your gobs, you howling hyenas," the miner shrieked.

"You shut it," I snapped back.

"Excuse me?" Mrs. Templeton straightened. Her mouth compressed, the tips of her nostrils whitening.

My breath hitched, and I pressed my hands to my cheeks. And this was why I didn't talk to ghosts anymore. *Weird Lenore, Crazy Lenore, Strange Lenore.* If I stayed out of the habit of talking to the dead, I wouldn't make mistakes like this so easily.

"Sorry," I said. "I didn't mean..." Snatching the map off the desk, I fled, and ran straight into Jonas, hovering outside. I reared backward.

His dark brows slashed downward. "I want to talk to you."

Chapter 7

MY HEART THUDDED AGAINST my ribs. I was safe. Jonas wouldn't hurt me. Not in broad daylight on Main Street with people around...

I looked toward the iron bench. The couple had abandoned it. My stomach dropped to the thick lawn. A butterfly flitted across the small lawn and landed on an orange lily. The flower swayed beside the stone hut.

The matchstick in Jonas's mouth swiveled. I tried not to stare at it, but its bobbing and weaving was hypnotic.

"How can I help you?" I winced. I'd sounded like a commission-only salesclerk.

Jonas's lanky form loosened. He scratched his cheek, looking less certain. "Uh, you found Abe." The matchstick jutted toward the information center's thatched roof.

My skin grew damp beneath my thin tunic. Jonas stood in the shade of an elm. I did not. My discomfort and that dancing matchstick evaporated my anxiety. Why were fraught moments frequently also ridiculous?

Keep it brief and to the point, and maybe he'll go. "Yes, I found his body."

"Where?" Arms folded over the denim jacket, he braced his shoulder against the round, stone building. The matchstick made a lazy circle.

"In Doyle Creek."

"Okay." Jonas crossed his ankles, the smooth sole of his boot aimed at me. "But where in the creek?"

"Off the Eastern Trailhead," I said. "You saw me there."

The miner stormed from the visitors' center, a pickaxe over his shoulder. He walked through me, and I shuddered at the deathly cold. The ghost didn't react. He either didn't see me, didn't see present-day Doyle, or didn't care.

Jonas nodded, his dark hair brushing the collar of his jacket. "It's a long trail. How far down it did you find him?"

I tore my gaze from the departing miner. "About a mile. There's a swimming hole."

"There's no swimming hole on that trail," he said.

"No," I said, starting to get annoyed, "off it." It figured the one guy in town a bigger outcast than me would glom onto me.

My gaze darted toward the street. People walked past, but none were cops. Not that I was in danger. I shifted my weight on the paving stones. I was safe. This was fine.

Jonas pulled the matchstick from his mouth and examined it, nose wrinkling. "And he was in the swimming hole? Drowned?"

My face tightened. "No, he was caught against a rock in the creek. It sort of goes past the swimming hole."

His eyes narrowed. "That water's got to be freezing. You're telling me you were swimming?"

Mary Hannon walked past with her friend Delaney, another childhood tormentor. The two looked at Jonas and me, and they laughed.

I gritted my teeth. I was an adult. I shouldn't care what others thought. "No, but there's a nice sandy area. I was... reading."

His narrow face flushed. "If he didn't drown, how'd he die?" He tossed the matchstick onto the thick patch of lawn.

"I don't know." Go *away*.

Jonas straightened off the stone wall. "When I asked if he drowned, you said *no*," he said accusingly.

A VW van roared past, pink flowers painted on its side. Exhaust clouded the small park, and I waved it away.

"I—I just meant I don't know how he died," I said, flustered. "He was in the water. Maybe he drowned. It looked like he'd... I don't know."

"You said he didn't drown," Jonas said stubbornly.

"I said I didn't... I don't know." Why was I telling Jonas anything? I didn't owe him answers. I *shouldn't* say anything. But I had answered because it was easier than asking questions, and I wanted him to leave.

"But you found him in the water, and he was dead?" He drew a fresh matchstick from the breast pocket of his denim jacket.

"Yes," I said, neck stiffening, "and what's with the matchsticks?"

Jonas grunted. "They keep me steady. What else did you see?"

"Why were you asking about Wharton yesterday at the trailhead?"

"Because Wharton and Abe got in a fight last Tuesday."

"A fight?"

"Abe shoved him. Wharton fell off the sidewalk and has been walking around with his arm in a sling and threatening to sue ever since. I've been avoiding him."

"Why?" I asked. "You didn't shove him."

"No, but I laughed when his ass hit the pavement."

"There were stickers, with strange symbols on them. They looked like—"

"What do I care about stickers?" Jonas's dark brows drew downward. "You see anything else?"

"No." Go.

"No? Just no?" he asked, tone mocking.

"NO." My voice boomed in my chest. It felt... good. A tourist couple strolling past turned to look, expressions curious.

Jonas's lip curled. "All right, Lenore. I'll be seeing you."

My jaw hardened. *Not if I have anything to say about it.*

He jammed the fresh matchstick into his mouth. Jonas turned and strode down the sidewalk.

I sagged. It was that damned matchstick's fault. It had distracted me. I'd told him everything, and though I'd learned a few things, I hadn't asked what Wharton and Abe had been fighting about.

What if Jonas *had* killed Abe? Now he knew exactly where Abe had been found, and there might be evidence there.

The police are investigating. They're looking for Jonas. They must *have collected any evidence at the swimming hole.*

But the police also thought Mira was a suspect. They weren't infallible.

If Jonas was headed to that trailhead... I hurried after him. He got into a blue Honda Civic missing its rear bumper. It was too far away to read the license plate.

I jogged across the street to my Volvo. Jonas peeled off, tires screeching, headed south, toward the highway.

I pulled from my spot. A tourist family crossed the street, delaying me. Once they were on the sidewalk, I made a U-turn as quickly as I dared and followed.

But by the time I reached the highway, the Honda had vanished. I hesitated at the stop sign. A logging truck rumbled past. I scraped my teeth across my bottom lip. *West toward Angels Camp or east toward Nevada and the trailhead?*

A red-tailed hawk flew in front of my windshield, close enough to see the definition of his feathers. I gasped. The bird zoomed upward and vanished above the pines.

The hawk had been heading east. And Jonas could do the most damage at the crime scene. "East it is," I muttered and turned onto the highway, my back toward the setting sun.

I drove past lakes dotted with granite islands graying in the twilight. The parking lots were near empty, swimmers and boaters gone to their dinners. I scanned every lot for Jonas's car, worried I'd chosen the wrong direction.

When I reached the east trailhead, I saw the blue Honda. Relieved, I turned into the lot and parked. The Honda was parked where Abe's van had been. The police must have impounded the van.

Jonas was nowhere in sight. But there was really only one place he could be—on the trail. Calling the Sheriff's Department, I asked for Deputy Denton.

"May I ask why, young lady?" a woman asked, arch.

I flushed. She probably thought I was calling because I had a crush on Owen Denton, which I did.

"Tell him Jonas—" I didn't know his last name. *Oh well.* "Jonas's Honda is on the east trailhead. He's not in it. Here's his license plate." I rattled off the plate. "Got that? I think he's headed to the swimming hole where Abe Crowe's body was found."

She repeated it back to me. "Now, young lady—"

I disconnected before she could ask me why I thought he was headed to the crime scene. But Jonas *must* have gone to the swimming hole.

I studied the empty Honda. My stomach burned. If he found evidence there and destroyed it, that was on me.

Jonas couldn't have gone far though. Swallowing, I stepped from the car. If he confronted me, I'd just tell him the truth—that I'd called the cops and they knew we both were here.

It was a reckless move—one I wouldn't take today. But spying on him seemed logical at the time.

I didn't plan to confront him, just follow him and let the cops know if he destroyed evidence. I wouldn't even interfere with that. Though I'd take pictures of him doing it, if I could do it safely.

And I was still young enough to think I was immortal.

Grabbing my copper water bottle off the seat, I strode toward the trailhead, with its two stone markers. Behind them, the beginnings of a soft, California sunset had begun, the clouds turning to fat cherry blossoms.

I stepped onto the trail and cocked my head, listening. I didn't hear anyone. I didn't want Jonas to surprise me. Cautiously, listening hard, I moved about twenty feet above the trail.

I hiked roughly parallel to the trail, glancing down the hill to make sure I wasn't going off course. I couldn't see the path itself, but I could see the spot where the hillside dropped and vanished to make room for it. If Jonas was on it, I'd see the top of his head—hopefully before he saw me.

Twenty minutes later, I found the turn to the swimming hole. I stopped and listened. All I heard was the gentle babble of the creek.

I skidded down the hillside to the trail. Taking the harder and quieter way over rocks and boulders, I made my way down the hill.

But soon it became obvious Jonas wasn't there. I clambered over boulders, searching, insides shrinking, but he hadn't come this way.

Retreating the way I'd come, I studied the trail in the evening's half-light. The only fresh prints on this part of it were my own. I frowned. Jonas hadn't come as far as the swimming hole. Where *had* he gone?

Slowly, I retraced my steps, looking for footprints. Finally, I found one—a smooth, oversized boot print, not too deep. Jonas?

I raised my head. More flattened prints marked the trail ahead of me.

I looked behind me. No prints.

I studied the edge of the trail. A mullein plant, its soft, wide leaves crushed, as if someone had stepped on it. Behind it, a deer trail wove up the hill. Jonas could have gone this way.

"What are you doing here?" a man asked.

I started, dropping my phone, and whirled around.

The detective from Mira's shop stared stonily down at me.

Chapter 8

ON A WARM SUMMER night, there is no mountain gloom, only the soft unfolding of day into night. Even on moonless nights there's light from the stars, brilliant and low against the Sierra peaks.

Venus hung high in the sky. I'd swear I could see each of her seven points.

The detective, oblivious to the beauty, glared. "I asked what you're doing here."

"Hiking," I blurted and raised my water bottle as proof.

The detective mustn't have planned to go far. He wore a charcoal business suit and tasseled loafers to match.

"At this hour?" he asked. "After finding a body here, you're not scared?"

I really wished Owen Denton had come instead. Not because of my stupid crush—because I trusted Denton. I didn't trust Detective Vanning.

He smiled and clapped my shoulder. I staggered sideways on the trail. "Good job calling in Jonas Reed's car. You country girls are made of strong stuff, but you shouldn't have followed him alone."

"Doyle isn't the country," I pointed out, pedantically annoyed. But we were only two hours from Sacramento, and Doyle was the mountains.

"Whatever. You see him back there?" He angled his head toward the trail I'd just come up.

I shook my head. "No. If those are his tracks," *and they are,* "he didn't go any further than this point."

"Then what...?" He knelt beside the broken mullein and looked up the darkening hill. "You think Jonas went up there?"

"Yes."

He rose and winked. "I like you. No blather. You get to the point."

My neck and shoulders tightened. Many people confused introversion with stupidity. If Vanning thought I was falling for his compliments, he was one of them.

"How do you know Jonas?" the detective continued.

"I don't. I talked to him for the first time about an hour ago today," I said, voice taut.

"Talked to him about what?"

"He was asking about the body I found." And like a simpleton, I'd told him too much.

He smiled again. "Relax, kid. The local deputies told me you hike up here day and night."

I shifted my weight backward. What was Vanning getting at? "Yes?"

"I'd like your help, if you're up for it," the detective continued. "You think you can keep me on this trail?" He pointed up the hillside.

"I don't know. It's not much of a trail, and I've never been on it before."

"But?"

Did I *want* to help the detective? I didn't like him, but maybe I owed it to Abe's ghost. Maybe then he'd stay out of my dreams. I heaved a sigh. "But I can try."

"Good girl. Let's go." He started up the hill. His loafers slipped on loose earth, and he steadied himself.

My mouth compressed. *Good girl?* But I followed him up the hill despite my annoyance. On this rough trail, those dress shoes of his would be payback enough for his patronizing remark.

Detective Vanning looked to be in good shape, but it wasn't long before he was huffing. I smiled. Pale dust coated his shoes and the cuffs of his charcoal suit.

"It's the altitude." He panted. "I'm not used to it in Sacramento."

"What are you looking for?" I ventured, fiddling with my water bottle's canvas carrier. More stars had appeared, and the crescent edge of a gold moon peeped over the eastern horizon.

"Jonas's marijuana grove."

"I thought it belonged to Abe."

He grunted. "Maybe."

"This Jonas," I said, "does he have a record?"

"Petty theft. Drug dealing."

"Drugs?" I asked. *It keeps me steady.* Were the matchsticks a way for Jonas to manage an addiction?

"We've been tracking a special strain of marijuana with psychedelic properties."

I blinked. Mira had been the one to tell him about the "special" marijuana. If Detective Vanning had already known about it, he'd done a good job of masking it in his voice.

"I didn't think marijuana had psychedelic properties. Not that I've ever tried it," I added quickly.

He glanced over his shoulder at me and grinned. "It doesn't. That's why this stuff comes at a premium. We think they've been adulterating it somehow."

"And it comes from... Doyle?"

The detective stopped and pulled a sticker from the pocket of his charcoal blazer, handed it to me. "Recognize this?"

I sucked in a breath. "They were floating around Abe's body."

"It's the brand logo for that strain of marijuana."

Ansuz and Eiwaz, spiritual insight and altered states of consciousness. "Is the marijuana... dangerous?"

"The new stuff is all stronger, this more than most, and more dangerous to some people than others." Vanning stopped and braced his fists on his slim hips. "Are we still on the trail?"

I looked around. "You just stepped off it. It jogs this way." I pointed left.

"Sharp eyes." He huffed and changed direction.

I had to call out to him twice more when he started going wrong. We reached a ridge and sped up, the trail widening. The moon rose higher, brightening the trail.

"What about Abe Crowe's ex-wife? Does she... know?"

"Yeah, I talked to her yesterday in Addis Ababa."

"Where?"

"Ethiopia. She's finding herself in Africa."

"Right." Then she probably hadn't been involved in Abe's death.

Chest heaving, the detective stopped beside a pine and loosened his tie. "Didn't we pass this tree before?"

Wind had gnarled the pine into a twist and bent it at a right-angle to the sky. I frowned. It *did* look familiar. "We're on the ridge." I took a drink and rubbed my lips. "We can't be going in circles."

"I know, but I'm sure I saw that tree..." Vanning shook his head. "What do I know? Trees all look alike."

I frowned, blinking rapidly. No, they didn't. Each tree was unique as each person. That's what made them beautiful.

We kept walking. More stars appeared beside Venus, but the rising full moon had dimmed her light.

Twenty minutes later, I stopped beside a pine, twisted by the wind with a right-angle bend to the sky. "Something's... wrong." I cleared my throat.

"Like you said, we're still on the ridge." Vanning yanked off his tie. Folding it, he stuffed it into the pocket of his blazer.

"But that's the same tree."

"Can't be. We haven't gone off trail. We can't be going in circles."

And yet it was the same tree. I *knew* it was the same tree, and I drew a slow breath. I was tired now, too tired to strain to sense things, so I relaxed, letting my vision blur.

The atmosphere seemed to tighten, grow denser, as if the molecules in the air were expanding, pressing against each other, crushing the air from my lungs. I pulled my arms closer, clutching them to my chest, my dread growing.

Cold fingers trailed up my spine, electric, raising the hair on my arms. I scanned the clear sky, my breath quickening. A charge was building, and I thought uneasily about lightning strikes on clear days. A cloud miles away could do the job.

Vanning's mouth moved, and I raised a hand to my ear. His words were warped, as if he were speaking through water. We were alone on the ridge, and something, something, something was *wrong*.

And then we weren't alone.

Crystal balls of light rose smoothly from the mountainside. I stood frozen, dumbstruck by their unearthly beauty. Pale with blue-tinted edges they floated upward.

"Beautiful," I whispered, but no sound emerged from my throat.

A chill wormed through me. *No, not beautiful.*

They *should* have been beautiful, but they were cold, cold, cold, and I knew that I wasn't simply observing the orbs. My wonder turned to horror, my flesh crawling.

The orbs were aware. They were observing *us*, and their gaze was malignant.

I wanted to move but I couldn't. I wanted to speak, but my breath choked my throat. I felt how weak I was, how pathetic I was to still care about the Mary Hannons of the world. Those worries were meaningless, and so was I.

A silent moan escaped my lips. One orb floated closer, then another. Icy fear coated my skin. I didn't know what would happen if they touched us, but the thought of that touch filled me with revulsion.

I tried to look at the detective, but even my gaze was locked as firmly as my jaw. I prayed, and I wasn't sure to whom or for what. We were trapped, and the orbs were getting closer.

A hawk screamed.

The air lightened, and the globes of light blinked out of existence. The sense of watchfulness, of evil, remained though, and I gulped a shuddering breath.

Vanning gave a shout. A deer plunged across the trail and down the hill, scattering pebbles and loose earth.

Half a dozen deer followed her. We were just two small, insignificant people, alone again on a mountain against the expanse of night sky.

Detective Vanning pressed a hand to his chest and laughed. "The deer startled me."

I nodded. *The deer, yes.* But had he felt what I'd felt? Seen what I'd seen? "Did you see—?"

"Ball lightning. Cool phenomena. Never seen it before."

Lightning. I pursed my lips, a weight filling my gut. It was the logical explanation. I didn't like it.

Lightning or... something worse. The somethings I'd worked to block from my sight. The things that sometimes appeared at the corners of my vision. The things that weren't ghosts—strange floating tentacled orbs, creatures in top hats and plague doctor masks.

If all I saw were ghosts, maybe being a medium wouldn't be such a bad thing. But I saw so much more.

The detective had seen the orbs too though. I hadn't been hallucinating. That should have been a relief. It wasn't.

"Hey." Vanning shone the beam of his flashlight down the other side of the hill.

My tongue tasted sandpaper. "What is it?"

"Stay there." He plunged down the hill, his dress shoes slipping on the loose scree, and stopped on a ledge a half dozen feet off the trail.

I aimed my phone light. The silhouette of Detective Vanning squatted beside a small, still shape.

I pressed my hands to the front of my tunic. "No," I whispered. We hadn't found Jonas. We'd found Mira.

Chapter 9

Mira was dead.

Mira was dead, and my aunt clattered in the kitchen below. Pulling pans from low cupboards and shutting their doors. Setting her cooling coffee mug on the counter. Lifting it and setting it down again.

I tried to swallow down the nausea twisting its way up my throat. Mira was dead, and our lives were going on.

Mechanically, I dressed in a lightweight ivory tunic and matching slacks and walked to the window. In my aunt's back yard, a red-tailed hawk perched in an oak. Morning sunlight streamed through its branches. Life moved on.

I'd *known* Mira. She hadn't been a friend to me—more of a good acquaintance. But her death hurt.

It was worse for Ellen though. They'd been real friends.

Throat aching, I'd told Ellen the news last night. My aunt had sat, unmoving, in her favorite living room chair. I'd wanted her to cry. I'd wanted to comfort her. I'd wanted to hear her say *something*.

Instead, she'd put down her history book and walked to her bedroom at the rear of the house.

From the living room, I'd heard her bedroom door close. I'd heard a single sob. I'd crept to her door, listening, wondering if I should knock. But all I'd heard was silence and the ticking of the hallway clock.

I hadn't knocked.

The police had a warrant out for Jonas Reed's arrest now. I'd heard Detective Vanning request it on the hillside.

Jonas had gone into the forest. Mira had gone into the forest. Mira hadn't survived, and Jonas was missing, on the run.

In the oak, the hawk turned his head to face me. Hastily, I stepped from the window and pulled an ivory scarf from a basket on my dresser. A print of pale green ivy twined across its thin fabric.

Jonas was the logical culprit. He'd worked with Abe. Maybe he'd wanted to take over the marijuana operations. And he'd been in the area when Mira had been killed. *Logical.*

Heartbeat heavy, I ran the thin cotton scarf through my hands. But Mira hadn't seemed afraid of Jonas. She'd been afraid of someone though when that cop had loomed in the doorway.

I didn't tell.

Now Mira would never get a chance to tell. Legs leaden, I descended the stairs to the kitchen. I stopped in the open doorway. Ellen stood facing the pale green cupboards, arms bent at her sides.

She turned, expression bleak, cradling her coffee mug in her hands. "You're up."

"I'm so sorry about Mira."

My aunt looked down at her bare feet. Her toenail polish was chipped. The polish had always surprised me. Ellen seemed too nature oriented for pedicures.

"It's my fault," I said, and an ache grew at the back of my throat. "Mira was hiding something, and I didn't tell anyone yesterday."

"What?" Ellen's face darkened. Her knuckles whitened on the white mug.

I told her about the scene in her shop, about what Mira had said, about the detective. "If I'd told someone—"

"No. That's... No. What you heard... It could have meant anything."

That was a generous interpretation, and one I *wanted* to be true. But it didn't change the facts.

I could have gone straight to the Sheriff's Department after talking to Mira and told them my suspicions. I could have waited outside Mira's shop for Detective Vanning. I hadn't done either of those things.

Ellen set her mug on the counter and gripped my arms, shaking me slightly. "You're not to blame. If Mira had a secret, she should have said something. This isn't on you. You couldn't have known..." She trailed off, her eyebrows gathering in.

"I'm sorry," I said.

"I am too," she said in a low voice and released my arms, stepping away. "But I'm sorry for me, for losing a friend. I'm not sorry for her. Mira's troubles are over."

Briefly, I closed my eyes. I wanted to know, to understand. Understanding what had happened couldn't turn back time though. "Did she... have many troubles?"

"Just one, one that she never told me about. But I could see it in her aura. And I never pushed her on it either. Maybe Mira and I are both a little to blame." Ellen retrieved her mug and took a meditative sip.

I sat on the barstool in front of the butcher block island. "Why *didn't* you ask?"

"Because we all deserve our privacy." Ellen met my gaze. "Until we're in danger. And then, it's time to talk."

My pulse jumped. She wasn't talking about Mira anymore. "I'm not in danger."

"You most certainly were in danger up on that hill." She jerked her head toward the window above the sink.

"I was with Detective Vanning."

"Who was a fool to take you." Ellen's blue eyes flashed. "I don't understand you. You're afraid to see ghosts, so you neglect your mediumship practice. But you're not too afraid to go up on a mountain alone with a virtual stranger?"

"He's a *detective*."

"Just because he has a badge doesn't mean he's safe. And what about Jonas? He could have done anything. You can't *do* these things. You're not—" Ellen's lips clamped together. She strode to the sink and dumped her coffee.

"Not what?"

My aunt faced me. "Not seeing the big picture. I know you're an adult now. But I promised your father I would take care of you." She blinked rapidly and looked away.

I knew she wasn't being honest—she'd meant to say something else. "What aren't you telling me?" I asked quietly.

"Abe was selling drugs. I just want you to stay out of that scene."

"I know he was selling marijuana," I said slowly. "He grows it somewhere up in the mountains."

Ellen's head jerked back. She turned away. "Where did you hear that?"

"From Detective Vanning."

This wasn't right. None of this was *right*. Ellen was hiding something, and I didn't think it had to do with a stupid marijuana grove.

"That detective is far too free with his information," she said tartly.

"You don't trust me," I said. I wasn't angry. I didn't feel betrayed. I felt sad, and a dark, gray woolly mass unfurled in my chest.

Ellen shook her head. "That's not true."

"It's okay. You don't have to tell me everything going on in your life. Like you said, we all deserve our privacy." But the mass expanded, choking my throat.

"Lenore, no. What's happened is ugly and awful. I only want to protect you."

"I know." I studied my bare feet.

A breeze through the open kitchen window rustled the drying herbs over the island. It carried the clear mountain scent of summer—a scent Mira would never enjoy again.

"And… trying to protect you is wrong," Ellen said, surprising me again. "You're twenty-five, not a child."

We were quiet a long moment.

"It doesn't matter anymore." I slumped forward on the barstool. "The police are looking for Jonas."

"But you don't think they should be."

My head jerked up. "You saw that in my aura," I said, accusing.

Ellen shrugged. "I can't help it. I suppose I can turn it off and on, but it's become such a habit… I'm not *trying* to spy on you."

That felt true, and a measure of my dismay evaporated. I hooked the tops of my ankles on the barstool rungs. "Do you think Jonas is guilty?"

"I don't know. The fact is, I don't know much about any of it. It's such a tangle."

"Is it?" I asked. "It seems fairly straightforward to me. Jonas probably wants that marijuana grove. It's a case of partners in crime gone wrong."

"I can see you don't believe that though." She shook her head. "Not your aura—I can hear it in your voice."

"I'm not sure what to believe." But I was glad she was asking me. The comfortable closeness that had been missing between us for so long returned. My limbs loosened, and I relaxed on the stool.

But I hesitated, unwilling to shatter this new sense of peace. "Why...? Why do you think it's a tangle?"

Ellen exhaled slowly. "Abe was more than a gadfly. Everyone knew he was responsible for the tree spiking. It put the local loggers in danger. And some people supported his... activism."

"Supported him... financially?" I braced my elbows on the butcher block island.

She nodded.

"Like who?"

"Not Mira," Ellen said quickly. "But some of the other townsfolk. It led to real strain with the loggers. They're putting their lives on the line in an already dangerous profession."

"What other townsfolk?"

"It's kept quiet, for obvious reasons. But Mira had her suspicions. Her brother was a logger, so she paid attention, and she liked to forage in the woods for many of her herbs and mushrooms."

"Suspicions of whom?" I pressed. "Who was funding Abe?"

"Janice Price, Wharton Van Goethe—"

Pressing one hand to the island, I rose from the stool. "Wharton?"

"Yes, why?" Ellen plucked her mug from the counter and raised it to her lips. She noticed it was empty and refilled it.

"I saw him yesterday at the sawmill. It sounded like he wanted to buy Caleb's lumber company."

"That... might explain why he was financing the tree spiking up on Caleb's property. The trouble could drive down the price."

And after Wharton bought the lumber company—*if* he bought it—if word got out that he was behind the tree spiking, the loggers would revolt.

I nodded, curt, body heat rising. Wharton had motive.

Chapter 10

HOT ANGER BLOSSOMED IN my chest. Anger at Mira's death. Anger that my aunt was still hiding something from me. Anger that Abe Crowe had haunted my dreams again last night.

Alas, I hadn't figured out yet that I didn't make the best decisions when I was mad. Worse, I still thought I was invincible.

Wharton had motive. Mira *must* have suspected Wharton. Had she confronted him, and he'd killed her?

If I wanted to learn about Wharton's possible role in this, the best person to ask would be his victim, Caleb Morse. I got in my Volvo and returned to the sawmill and lumberyard.

When I entered the small store, Caleb wasn't behind the counter. A clerk I didn't recognize, with narrow eyes and thick glasses, phoned him for me. A palm-sized, carved wooden beaver sat by his elbow.

The clerk hung up. "The boss'll be here shortly." He eyed me curiously. "Not looking for lumber then?" Outside, the saw whined.

"No," I said and flushed for no good reason. I wished I could get past my shyness, but I didn't know how. Was practice really the answer? It sounded too easy.

After a few minutes of awkward standing around, Caleb strode into the lumber store, sawdust flaking his sandy hair. He grimaced. "This way." He angled his head toward the door and walked back out.

I followed Caleb up the sawmill's set of wooden steps and to an office at the back of the building, away from the noise of the saw blade. He dropped into an executive chair behind a big wooden desk. Carved animals lined its front.

"Sorry I was so rough on you the other day," he said, gruff. "I thought—Antoine set me straight about you. He said there's no way you'd be involved in tree spiking."

"No, of course not." I stammered in the office doorway. "That could kill someone." *And thank you, Antoine.*

"What can I do for you?"

"I—I wanted to ask you about Wharton Van Goethe."

He rolled up the sleeves of his red plaid shirt. "Why?"

"How far do you think he might go to buy your lumber company?" I held my breath.

Caleb pulled a pocketknife and small block of wood from a desk drawer. He nodded toward a wood and faux-leather chair on the other side of the desk.

Taking it for an invitation, I sat, perching at the front of the chair. A wooden cat sneered at me from the desk's corner.

"That," he said, "is a thought-provoking question. Another is why are you so interested?" He peeled a strip of wood off the block, and I wondered if the whittling kept Caleb "steady," like the matchsticks did for Jonas.

I swallowed. "I was with the police when they found Mira Tate's body."

"Mira." Caleb sighed. "That must have been terrible for you." He dug out another chunk of wood. "Heard they arrested Jonas Reed for that this morning."

My stomach fluttered uneasily. Had they? I hadn't heard it. Was it over? I wanted it to be over. *And yet, and yet...*

"What do you care about Wharton and my lumber company?" he asked, eyes narrowing.

"It's just... If Wharton was financing Abe's tree spiking, he's partly responsible," I blurted, my voice catching. "Jonas may have committed the murders, sure, but..."

"*May* have?" Caleb said, voice low. "You don't sound so sure. What's that supposed to mean, Lenore?"

"I mean—everyone thinks he did. He's the obvious suspect..." Why did I resist thinking him guilty? Because he was an outsider? Easy to blame?

"But Wharton's got you curious?" Caleb laughed shortly, the knife pausing over the wood. "Wharton takes things too far. But you're not just talking about him now, are you?"

Was I taking things too far? I blundered on. "The thing is, Abe pushed him off a sidewalk last Tuesday. They were arguing... about something." Embarrassed heat flushed my veins. "That's how he hurt his shoulder... On Tuesday."

I waited. My hands clenched and unclenched in my lap. "The police... they need to know the whole truth. It needs to come out. All of it." *Why is he staring at me like that?*

Caleb's gaze bored into mine. "The whole truth, huh?" His knife stilled.

"That marijuana grove is on your property. You must feel... I don't know, caught up in it... Somehow."

He should *care* about what happened. It should matter—not just because Wharton was trying to steal his business, but because two people had died.

Caleb resumed whittling. The knife slipped, slicing his thumb.

"Your hand—"

"It's fine." He fumbled in his desk drawer and drew out a wad of tissues, wrapped it around his thumb.

I struggled to fill the silence, to come up with something else to ask, but all I could come up with was nonsense. "Where exactly did Abe spike the trees?"

Thick eyebrows drawing together, Caleb set the unfinished wood on his desk. "Around that spring where his marijuana grove was planted. He wanted to make sure none of my men touched it, even if it was on my property."

He straightened in his chair and shifted forward. "That spring feeds Doyle Creek. But if you're thinking Abe was killed there and his body floated downstream, there's no way. There are too many obstructions in that creek."

Were there though? Or was Caleb trying to shift the liability for the death off his property? "Maybe someone moved the body. Have the police been up there?"

His forehead wrinkled, his brows lowering. "Not yet."

"Where *is* the spring?"

"Not far." He jerked his head toward an industrial window, laced with chicken wire. "There's a trailhead here at the lumber yard."

"Are there other trails to it aside from this one?"

He shrugged one shoulder. "Probably."

Did the deer trail where we'd found Mira last night lead to the spring? "I'd like to see the spring, if I may."

"Why?"

I wasn't sure why the spring seemed so important. But everything seemed to come back to Abe's grove by that spring. Even Mira had mentioned it. *Blasphemy.*

Besides, with Jonas arrested, he was no longer a threat. He wouldn't be guarding the place.

"I'd—I'd like to see it," I repeated.

"It's not a dangerous hike, but it's never a good idea to hike alone," he said. "People disappear in these woods, you know."

"I'm not a tourist. I know these woods."

He hesitated. "All right. I'll call the cops and let them know you're headed up there looking for the grove." He grinned. "Maybe that will set a fire under that fancy detective's a... butt."

Caleb opened a drawer and pulled out a folded topographic map. "You know how to read one of these?"

"Of course."

He shook his head and marked an X on the map in red ink. "It's a two-mile hike from here, mostly uphill. You've got enough water?"

"In my car. There are no logging roads into the area?"

"Yeah, but you won't get your car in very far. There was a washout last winter, and part of the road collapsed. There's a trail behind the mill that leads up to it and will bypass the road. It'll be quicker to take that."

I nodded and took the map. "Thanks." I scanned the map. The deer trail where we'd found Mira wasn't on it, but the hillside was. It looked like you *could* get to the spring from that ridgeline.

"Maybe you should wait for the cops," Caleb said.

With Jonas arrested, I didn't know why they'd come, other than to see the grove for themselves. But why did I need to see it? "I'm surprised they haven't gone up there yet themselves. It's an illegal grove."

Caleb snorted. "That detective? He doesn't want to get his shoes dirty. That'll be a problem for the sheriff, when she gets back."

If she gets back. I shook myself. Of course the sheriff would return. But when you spend too much time in your head, it's easy to imagine disaster.

So why didn't I imagine the disaster I was about to walk into?

Chapter 11

A HIKE HAD NEVER been so easy.

That should have made me suspicious.

It was as if something was drawing me to the spring, pulling me up the mountain. The grade was steep, but my steps were light. I hurried onward, heedless of the stitch in my side, of my heaving chest, of my straining breath.

Any misgivings I might have had about this trek had vanished. My guilt over Mira's death was gone, and I didn't wonder about that.

My joy seemed normal. Later I could see it was odd, and I wondered if there might have been something supernatural in my eagerness. But that morning remains in my memory as the most magical of mountain summer days.

The meadows were thick with wildflowers. The air raced with life and the pungent scent of pine. Birds and chipmunks chattered on sun-warmed boulders below. Light streamed golden through the boughs above.

The warmth on my skin was delicious. The sun's energy rippled through me, charging my steps. The earth was alive, and for the first time—though not the last— I truly felt it, the thrum of her, the scent of her.

We tend to think of nature as something outside us. We go to nature. We visit it, bask in it. But that afternoon, I understood viscerally that I was connected to it. I was—all of us are—part of nature too.

My heart was open, my mind expansive. Everything was possible and good, and I was giddy with delight.

Then, beside a massive pine, my summer sense of wild freedom abruptly ended. I was a foolish young woman again, sweaty and out of breath, hair plastered to my neck.

And I wasn't alone.

The miner's ghost, pick ax slung over one shoulder, muttered along the trail behind me. *There's gold here. I know it, I know there is. Got to be gold. I kin smell it. There's gold here. I know it, know there is...*

His words cycled in an endless loop. I bit back my annoyance. Had he been like that during his life, using the chant to propel himself forward? Or was he a looping ghost, doomed to repeat the same words and actions over and over?

But he didn't seem to be looping on the trail. He kept hiking steadily upward behind me.

Exasperated, I finally stepped off the trail and let the ghost pass. He continued ahead of me for a good quarter mile then vanished between two pines.

The forest felt lonelier without him, though there was plenty of life on the trail. Purple flowers bloomed through cracks in granite. A chipmunk raced across the path and scampered up a pine. A mosquito buzzed around my head. I swatted at it.

Breathing heavily, I stopped to consult the topographical map. My muscles relaxed. I was still on track. I took a swig of water and continued on.

On a mountainside, you have to pay attention to your footing. There are boulders to scrabble over and fallen pines to clamber around. There are creeks to forge and gullies to cross and sudden clearings to catch your breath in.

I hiked onward. The forest quieted, sounds falling away to leave only that of my breathing and my footsteps. The miner's ghost appeared behind me.

There's gold here. I know it, I know there is. Got to be gold. I kin smell it. There's gold here. I know it, know there is...

Letting him pass, I stopped again to consult the map. I frowned. I hadn't gone off trail, but...

I cursed. Had I gone in a circle? I'd swear I'd passed this Ponderosa with the missing bark before.

From my vantage, I couldn't see the mountain's ridge line, and I *should* be able to see it. Which meant... I'd gone off course somewhere.

My frustration turned to worry. I adjusted the pack on my back.

I retraced my steps.

Got to be gold. I kin smell it. There's gold here. I know it, know there is... The dead miner rambled behind me.

Thirty minutes later, we were at the same Ponderosa with missing bark. I rubbed the back of my damp neck.

It was the same tree. Every tree really was unique. The pine's missing bark was shaped a bit like a garden gnome with a fat belly and pointed hat.

The miner continued up the hill. I walked closer to the pine to take a picture and sucked in a breath. Someone had carved a faint symbol into the raw wood—Abe's rune.

Abe must have left it as a trail marker to his grove. I was on the right track, and my steps lightened.

Relieved, I continued upward through the trees. The miner reappeared. I stopped in front of the same Ponderosa.

I blinked. It *had* to be a different tree. Because I'd been going consistently upward. I *couldn't* be hiking in circles.

And yet... That gnome-shaped section of missing bark... It was the same. I'd swear it. And the same thing had happened last night on the hill with the detective, before we'd found Mira... Bile rose in my throat.

I collected three pinecones from the needle-covered ground. Setting them in a pyramid between the tree's thick roots, I continued on.

The miner reappeared behind me. *There's gold here. I know it, I know there is. Got to be gold. I kin smell it. There's gold here. I know it, know there is...*

"Will you talk about something else?" I shouted.

A trio of crows shot from a nearby pine. The ghost continued past me. I drank more water and glared at his retreating figure.

I started to follow him, then froze. The ghost had been behind me, but he'd been in *front* of me before.

The miner was looping.

A sour smell—the sweat on my skin—rose around me. If the ghost was looping, so was I.

Was I dead? Was I a ghost?

I swayed and braced my hand against a nearby pine. I didn't *feel* dead. I could remember what I had for breakfast. I could remember what got me here. But what did ghosts remember?

I straightened. Bits of dirt flecked my palm. Slowly, I brushed them off. I had interacted with the tree, collecting dirt on my palm. I didn't think ghosts could do that.

But that was the problem. I scrubbed a hand over my face, my throat tightening. I didn't *think*, because I didn't *know*. I didn't know about the habits of ghosts, because I hadn't studied them.

I'd been lazy. Lazy learning about things that affected me. Lazy about my life.

I should be able to talk to people more easily. I should know what to say and when to say it. I should have a job I *liked*. But retreating into Tolkien and other stories had been easier.

"But I'm not dead," I whispered. And then more loudly, "I'm not dead."

Swallowing, I checked the map and continued up the hill. I stopped at a ponderosa pine with missing bark and a faint carved rune.

My pulse turned sluggish. Three pinecones lay in a pyramid between its roots.

Chapter 12

I WASN'T DEAD. I *couldn't* be dead.

My heart thundered clumsily in my chest. Not *dead*. My breath grew loud. Not *dead*. And yet I was looping up the mountain, just like that miner.

My nails pressed into my palms, and they hurt. I closed my eyes. *Not dead. Not dead not dead not dead.*

I wasn't dead, but I wasn't right either. Something was badly wrong, and running up the same trail again wasn't going to solve it.

I leaned against the pine and inhaled slowly. *Think.*

I could try a new direction... and possibly get lost. But I had the map, and I knew how to read it. I *shouldn't* get lost.

Without much hope, I checked my phone. *No service.* That was common in the mountains. It was common in *Doyle.* I was on my own.

Swallowing, I studied the map and struck off in a southerly direction.

Twenty minutes later, the pine with the missing gnome-shaped bark rose into view. My legs turned to stone.

I wasn't dead. I'd done something different. And yet... I'd looped back to my starting point again. A tremor wracked my body. My hands gripped the straps of my pack. *Observe, don't absorb.*

Okay, what am I observing? I was not lost. I was not walking in circles, because the first time I'd been constantly going uphill, and the second time... well, I hadn't been going in circles.

So, if I wasn't lost, and I wasn't dead, something else was happening. *What?*

Magic. Dread spiraled in my gut, because if it was magic...

I could hear Ellen's voice in my mind, a past lecture. *Magic has its own logic, but the logic is* there. *That's why you need to study it, that, and someday, you'll need it. Not all magic is used for good, and you need to be prepared...*

But I hadn't studied magic. I'd avoided it. Chin quivering, I turned in place, looking for a new path.

The miner plodded up the hill toward me. I swallowed, mouth dry. If I was a medium, now was the time to use that talent.

I cleared my throat. "Excuse me."

He walked past, unheeding.

I trotted after him. "Pardon me, I mean, can you hear me? I'm trying to find a spring." I had to jog to keep up with his long strides. "I'm lost. Can you hear me?"

He vanished beside a twisted pine in a small clearing.

So... That hadn't worked.

I squatted, my back against the pine. What would Ellen do?

When in doubt, go inward and listen. It was another of Ellen's sayings. My jaw tightened. My gaze flicked to the pine branches above me. "Ellen, I'm listening now. Maybe too late, but I'm listening."

I shut my eyes. *Listen.*

A faint wind rivered in the pines above me. My breath was loud and too fast. My heart pounded in my chest like a shaman's drum.

Like a shaman's drum.

I breathed more deeply, and the beat slowed. *Listen.*

I listened to the drum of my heart. Its rhythm steadied. The drum was there, and I was *alive*.

Pine needles crunched on the forest floor. Something—or someone—was moving toward me, and I stilled. My breath quickened. The steps came closer. I opened my eyes.

A deer stood in the clearing. She studied me, her huge eyes unblinking, and I closed my eyes again.

The deer was still there.

She was *there*. I could see her as clearly as if my eyes were open, but they weren't open, they were closed, and she was surrounded by darkness.

The doe turned and took two steps away from me. Her tail flicked. She looked back, as if saying, *Well? Aren't you coming?* She moved off.

In my mind's eye, I scrambled to my feet. I followed her into the darkness.

Blackness pressed in on me, and I hesitated. The deer glimmered, moving ahead, surefooted. I walked forward. Every now and then, she would look back, as if assuring herself I was still there. We kept going. We were descending now.

Lights danced at the edges of my vision. Another sound tickled my attention—burbling water. Shapes emerged from the darkness. Silhouettes of pines, strong and straight as soldiers. More delicate, lazy shadows of ferns.

Color poured in like swirling paint, and I stood at the edge of a spring. Water rippled from a break in a stone, splashing into the pond, which poured itself out into a stream. Rectangles of white floated in the stream and dotted the banks.

The doe bent her head to drink, then tossed her head and stepped away from the pond. I squatted and reached into the pond, retrieving one of the rune stickers. I stared into the water. Sawdust eddied in its depths.

A nearby section of mud at the spring's edge was churned by boots, and then there was a flattening of the mud, as if a sled had been dragged through stands of marijuana plants.

I followed the drag marks and boot prints down the hill until they vanished amidst the dead pine needles. A hawk screamed above me, and I glanced up into pine branches. I squinted, shielding my eyes against the burst of light.

I was leaning against the pine in the real world again. My eyes were open. A hawk circled lazily above me.

Shakily, I exhaled. I knew where the spring was now. I knew it as if I'd visited it daily. Rising, I walked up the hill. I didn't look at the map. I *knew*.

And whatever magic had kept looping me to the same pine had no hold over me now.

I descended into a gully, and there it was. The marijuana. The ferns. The pines. The spring. The boot prints, their treads deep and well defined.

I compared them to the photo on my phone. They looked a lot like those at Abe's van. I punched the air, elated. Abe had been here.

But there were no stickers. I scanned the clear water. None.

A gust of wind tossed the pines. Something white flickered at the edge of my vision.

Numbly, I walked to a fern and knelt. A sticker lay in the mud, and I picked it up, uncovering a small, imprint in the earth. It was as clear as a clay mold and in the shape of a crow.

I rose. Drag marks led from the spring, through the stands of marijuana, and down the hill. The marks vanished in the pine needles littering the forest floor.

My triumph fled, replaced by damp heaviness. If Abe had been killed here and dragged away, to a wider part of the creek, where he would float downstream and eventually be found...

But his van had been at the trailhead. If Abe had been killed here, his van had been driven to the Eastern Trailhead by the killer. The boot prints at his van hadn't been Abe's. They'd belonged to his killer.

I closed my eyes. Of course they hadn't been Abe's. He'd been wearing loafers, not boots with deep treads.

Why move the body? To make it appear he'd died farther downstream?

There was only one person who'd want to move the scene of the crime. I scraped my fingers across my head. If the police came up here, they might find trace evidence.

If?

A crow... And suddenly I knew. My hands trembled. I clutched my arms to my chest. The police weren't coming.

"Lenore." Caleb Morse walked down the hill toward me. "What's that in your hand? Did you find what you were looking for?"

I tensed. Caleb hadn't called the police. Caleb was a killer.

Chapter 13

HAIRS LIFTED ON THE nape of my neck. The sound of the wind in the pines mingled with the rushing of the creek. Fear slithered across my skin, cool and acrid.

Wharton couldn't have killed Abe. With his shoulder damaged, he wouldn't have had the strength. I'd *seen* the fight Abe had put up before he'd died.

Caleb had killed Abe and Mira. He'd had a better motive to kill Abe than anyone—Abe was the one spiking his trees. And opportunity? This was Caleb's property. He could come and go as he pleased.

The crow imprint had come from one of his carvings. It had been pressed into the mud, maybe stepped on during the struggle with Abe.

And now Caleb was here to kill me. I hadn't told anyone I was coming up here, and neither had Caleb. *Idiot!*

"Oh, hey, it's you," I said brightly, and my voice didn't crack. "Just a second, I forgot something." I turned and jogged down the hill, my hiking shoes skidding on loose pine needles.

The breeze carried the scent of butterscotch from the Ponderosas and the harsh stench of Caleb's sweat. I glanced over my shoulder. I'd put more space between the two of us, but Caleb was tramping after me.

I ran.

I pelted down the steep hillside, gravity hurrying me along, my strides lengthening. It was a dangerous, maniacal run, slipping on pine needles and loose rocks, guaranteed to meet disaster. And it did.

My feet flew from beneath me. By some stroke of luck, instead of tumbling headfirst, I fell backward.

I shot down the hillside, rocks clawing at my arms and legs. I grabbed a passing pine with my free hand. It snapped my arm straight, yanking it in its socket, but I stopped, heart galloping.

Caleb's booted feet thudded above me. My shoulder screaming, I leapt up and kept going, side stepping, skidding, slewing down the hillside.

And still his footsteps came. My shoulder throbbed. I was lost. I had no idea where I was. All I knew was that I was headed down.

My pale clothing was a benefit if a rescuer was searching for me, but now a killer was doing the looking. I stood out amid the dark trees like the proverbial sore thumb.

Someone help me. Someone help...

A hawk cried above me, but I didn't dare glance up. I ran with no destination in mind except to get away. No one would help me. I would die here, and the certainty of my death settled in my chest.

And then I *saw.*

My consciousness flew high above the mountain. I shouldn't have been able to distinguish any detail, but I saw through the eyes of a hawk now. I saw my pale-clothed figure racing down the hill and Caleb following.

I was still me and running down that mountain. But my consciousness, the me that remained outside myself, was bigger.

I knew things I shouldn't have known.

I knew my aunt was home with a bad feeling. I knew Caleb's determination to keep me on the mountain permanently. I knew Detective Vanning was at the sheriff's station, annoyed he was *still* stuck in podunk Doyle.

I knew every inch of the hill. I knew that past the slight rise on my left there was a massive pine, its roots dangling over a gully. I knew the gully was big enough to hide me.

I knew love.

It filled me, a warm, expansive glow beyond all description. And in that moment, I wasn't afraid.

Then I was back in my body, a stitch growing in my side, gripping my shoulder, gasping for breath. I veered left and over the rise. Bent double, I ran up its low slope. I sped past the massive pine and dropped, skidded, collapsed into the gully.

As I fell, I twisted and grabbed the dangling roots. I hauled myself beneath the dirt overhang, heedless of my aching shoulder.

Caleb's footsteps thundered closer. God help me, I closed my eyes, jaw clenched.

He ran past.

I didn't move. Didn't breathe.

His footfalls receded. Waiting until I couldn't hear them anymore, I scrabbled from my hiding place. I descended through the gully. When it flattened out, I jagged right, in the opposite direction from Caleb.

I didn't bother heading downward; I just wanted away. But I couldn't keep up this pace. I slowed.

There was a heavy, animal snort, and I started. The doe appeared, trotting at my side, and I caught my second wind. When she veered down the hillside, I followed, but my jog soon turned to a stagger.

We were on the north face of the hill now and deep in mountain shadows. The pines gave way to a patchwork of bare earth and snow on scree, the loose bits of dark, jagged rock broken down by wind and rain.

The deer stopped beside a wide strip of white. She looked toward me, then toward the snow.

I walked onto it, my hiking shoes crunching through its thin, icy crust. Though I was in the open, I'd be harder to spot here, and hope jolted through my body. Finally, my clothes made decent camouflage.

I descended through the snow, slipping here and there until I reached more scree. Scree was harder to traverse than snow, but it was what I had.

Hawk shrieked, a shadow passing above my head. He bulleted down the mountain ahead of me.

I followed the bird's path. I didn't question that I was now following the animals. At this point, I didn't know where I was. Straight down was as good a path as any.

I started across the scree. It slid and clattered beneath me, and I winced at the noise.

"Hey!" Caleb shouted.

I looked behind me. He jogged into the snow after me.

I moved more quickly, falling to my butt, scraping my hands on the sharp rocks. I kept on, gritting my teeth against the pain in my shoulder.

Caleb moved faster. "Get back here!"

"What do you want?" I shrieked, not slowing.

"I saw you talking to that cop last night. I know you saw me there. I won't be blackmailed."

I shook my head, my body temperature rising. "What?" *How could...?* Caleb must have still been on that hill when we'd found Mira. And my questions this morning... He thought I'd been hinting at blackmail? But I hadn't seen him.

"I *saw* you," he bellowed. "You looked right at me and turned away."

"I didn't see you!" But it didn't matter. It was too late. I knew the truth. "You killed them," I shouted. "You killed them both."

"Abe was destroying my business. What choice did I have?"

"You killed him at the spring and moved his body. You used his van to do it, and you had to break a window to get inside." There'd been no glass on the ground at the trailhead. That window had been broken somewhere else.

"The idiot had locked his own keys inside again. He drove it up the road to the spring and locked himself out." Caleb barked a laugh. "He actually asked me for a ride."

That explained how Caleb had gotten to me so quickly at the spring. He'd lied about the washed-out road.

"And Mira?" A charcoal-colored rock shot from beneath my feet. I fell to a crouch, my hands dropping to the stones beside me. Their sharp edges bit my palms.

"She was asking questions about Wharton. I sent her to the spring," he said, "just like you. I didn't think she'd find anything. But she found one of my carvings. A crow. It must have fallen out of my pocket when—"

"When you killed Abe?" I screamed, crab walking down the slope.

Scree rattled above me. He was too close.

"You're going to fall," he shouted. "There's a cliff ahead."

Maybe, maybe not. My vision—my knowing—of the terrain was gone. But I wasn't going to take Caleb's word for anything.

The clatter of scree above me grew louder. I tensed, my movements jerky, uneven.

Sharp, angular stones tumbled past. The sound of falling rock crescendoed.

Caleb shrieked. The mountainside was moving, and I was going with it, its skin of scree flowing like water.

Caleb screamed again, bulleting past me. He reached for my hand. Instinctively, I recoiled, twisting away, and he vanished.

He vanished.

I blinked, horrified. There *was* a cliff ahead. Caleb had gone over it. Rocks banged, echoing below me.

I floundered, trying to stop my descent. But the rock fall had me. There was nothing to hold that wasn't moving. Helpless, I scraped my heels against the scree. I clutched at nothing.

A fragile baby pine, no more than three feet high and thin as a rattler whipped past. I lunged, grabbed it with my uninjured arm. My feet met air. The tree bent. My legs skidded over the cliff. I clung to the tiny tree.

With a wrench, I grabbed it with my other arm. So at least my shoulder wasn't dislocated.

A stone struck the top of my head, and I cried out. More stones hit my shoulders. The sound was awful. The fragile tree kept its grip on the hillside. And then the clatter diminished.

I looked up, my lower body dangling over nothing. The deer stood where the scree met the snow. She bobbed her head and walked away, vanishing on the other side of the hill.

Chapter 14

"HOW IS SHE?" SHERIFF McCourt's voice was low in Ellen's kitchen.

I shifted guiltily outside the kitchen door, book in my arm. I shouldn't be eavesdropping again. But I'd come down the stairs and heard the two women there, and my feet hadn't wanted to move further.

I was just glad our regular sheriff had returned to duty. It felt like life was getting back to normal, but something had changed, and I didn't feel right.

Maybe that was why I'd stopped outside the kitchen door. Or maybe because I'd tossed and turned the last two nights, sleep evading me. Abe Crowe hadn't revisited my dreams, but Caleb went over that cliff again and again.

"Lenore's tougher than she looks," Ellen murmured.

I tucked the poem I'd written during my sleepless night into the book. Ellen's paperback on shamanism was forty years old, its cover bent and worn. I hoped its age meant it was more rather than less accurate. I needed all the help I could get.

Yesterday in the woods, the strange lights on the trail... My shamanism was coming for me, whether I liked it or not. I wasn't going to ignore it, even if it did mean working with the dead.

"We found more evidence at the spring," the sheriff said. "Caleb's tactical flashlight. It was dented and had Abe's blood and hair still on it."

"The murder weapon," my aunt breathed.

"Part of it. We think he hit Abe with it then held him under."

"Are you sure it was Caleb's?"

"It had his name on it," the sheriff said. "We found Mira's car at the lumberyard. It was well hidden, but we found it."

"What about the carving Lenore mentioned?"

"We found that too, with mud on it, and we found its imprint at the spring, clear as day. It all lines up."

"And Lenore won't be charged with anything?"

"No one thinks a girl Lenore's size shoved a man like Caleb off a cliff."

"No, but this is a small town. People will talk."

I slid the paperback from beneath my arm and gripped it one handed.

"Your niece isn't being charged," the sheriff said. "There's no reason to give her name out, if that's what's worrying you. As far as the public knows, she's an anonymous witness."

"Thank you," Ellen said.

I tiptoed from the house with the book. My Volvo was parked in the drive; the sheriff must have known I was home. Maybe she'd known I was listening at the kitchen door too. Muscles aching, I walked past my Volvo.

I hadn't even considered people might think I'd had something to do with Caleb's death. He'd been up on that mountain because of me. I didn't feel a bit of guilt. Remorse over my foolishness, yes. But no guilt.

I tilted my face to the sun and focused on the feel of its warmth, on the faint breeze on my skin. The anxiety that had gripped me since Caleb's death evaporated.

Inhaling deeply, I walked past homes spaced well apart. I walked past elms and pines. I walked past the park with its bandstand and to Main Street.

Stopping on the corner by the bookstore, I looked into the elm branches above me. Hawk perched on one.

"Thank you," I said. "Thanks to Deer as well, if you see her."

Hawk inclined his head. *Shaman.*

"*Am* I a shaman?"

You know the answer.

I knew—now—that shamans had to undergo a sort of dismemberment to come into their power. This could be literal, symbolic, or emotional. I felt like I'd gone through a bit of all three.

But at least I knew now I wasn't a medium. I touched my arm where the bird's talons had raked it. "I have a lot to learn," I said, "don't I?"

Hawk didn't reply.

"So, what next?" I asked.

Get a real job.

A dragonfly whisked past, so close I could hear the hum of its ir-ridescent wings. It made a drunken loop, shimmering cerulean, before vanishing over the false front of the bookstore. I smiled. Then I laughed. A pair of tourists glanced at me and gave me a wide berth, crossing the street.

I walked to the bookstore. The sign was still in the window.

I walked inside.

ℓℓ

Can't wait to read more? Grab *Bound*, book 1 in the Doyle Witch Fairy Queen Trilogy!

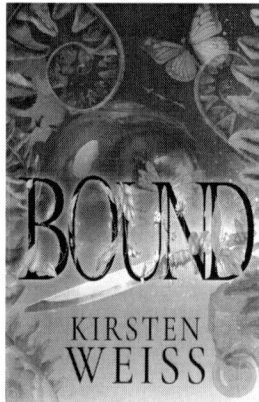

Bound by magic, bound by love, bound by murder...

The Bonheim triplets live seemingly ordinary lives, hiding their magic from their neighbors in the small, mountain town of Doyle, California. But then a body is found in flighty, big sister Jayce's coffee shop. Confronted by a sheriff with a grudge, a sister in denial, and a sexy lawyer with an agenda of his own, no-nonsense Karin must prove her sister innocent.

But as Karin works to unravel the murder, the knottier the mystery of her small mountain town becomes. Why are hikers vanishing in the nearby woods? Why are some people cursed with bad luck and others with good? And what is Jayce's lawyer hiding?

With her sister's fate hanging by a thread, Karin struggles to untangle the truth, and death stalks ever closer...

Knot magic spells at the back of the book!

Follow the magic with the Doyle Witch trilogy, starting with book 1, *Bound*. Each book has its own complete mystery and romance told from a different sister's point of view, and *Bound*, *Down* and *Ground* can all be enjoyed independently, with a magical storyline weaving through the three books.

If you're a fan of Charlaine Harris, Heather Blake, or Amanda M. Lee, don't miss *Bound*. Escape into the enchanting world of Doyle today.

Follow the magic with the Doyle Witch trilogy. **Click here** to get your copy of and escape into the enchanting world of Doyle today.

How to Become a Shaman

Cast off your dust-spoiled boots.
Unravel the ribbons from your hair.
Chant,
'Til your breath thrums you into trance.
Sing then to your old life, sing it bare,
And welcome the whirl of your new dance.

Leave your lantern, its light's too bright,
And step barefoot into moonlit canyons.
Follow the whispers of the pines at night,
To a deer skull, shimmering bone-white.
Scoop blackened earth into its gaping vaults,
Mugwort seeds into its dreaming eyes.
Drip dawn-cold dew into those hollows,
And ignite your dreams to touch the sky.

Drum with hawk and deer, hooves and wings.
Circle in a wild and wanton dance.
Leap and sway and spin 'til the world swings,
Until you fall, as if by chance.

Lie in the cradle of a plum tree's bower.
Sink through its silvery roots, tunneling deep.
Your heartbeat echoing your sure, steady steps.
Race through caverns to Lower World, and keep

Close counsel with the animal guides
Sipping tea from gilded chalices.
Listen to their stories, sharp as thorns.

Climb onto Raven's back,
Her feathers sleek as oil,
And ride through the dusk's dying flare.
Cling tight through the cloud's ashen coils,
And offer spring ivy to the hermit waiting there.

Gather sinew and fur, feathers and hair.
Take beads from a rusted button tin.
Weave them into a net, dark spirits to snare.
Wash your net in a snow-melt stream, ice on skin.
Now *you* are the guardian, woven of will and bone.

Pluck droplets of fog weighted with sorrow.
Seal them in a sleek glass jar, blue as midnight.
On a mist-washed night, pour them on a grave,
So the dead may drink deep and find the light.

Slide polished black boots onto your feet.
Knot velvet ribbons into your wild hair.
Reborn in starlight, dare new feats,
Your heart a wild and untamed lair.

Sneak Peek of Bound

ONCE UPON A TIME, in the foothills of granite mountains, when the sun hadn't yet risen in the east, there were three sisters. And one, me, had been stuck at the hospital all night.

The shadow of our small town's modern hospital loomed over the parking lot. Behind it swelled Sierra peaks, a jagged frame vanishing into dark clouds. The muggy air promised rain to come, but I shivered in my thin blouse and safari jacket.

Maybe if I hadn't been so tired, I would have paid more attention to the images written in the clouds, to the words whispering in the sough of the wind, sluggishly shifting the redwood branches.

But I wasn't looking for portents. I wanted relief. So I ignored the throb of wild expectation in the air that raised gooseflesh on my arms. I ignored the hooting of an owl after sunrise – a sure sign of death coming to the house. I ignored the coil of iridescent purple oil in a nearby puddle that shaped itself into a grinning skull.

I yawned and shuffled car keys between my fingers. Eyes hot with exhaustion, I leaned against my Ford Fusion, grimaced and pulled away. The car was covered in droplets of moisture. Now, so was I.

A crow flapped overhead and cawed. It settled on the branch of a redwood tree and regarded me with one beady black eye.

My keys slipped, jingling, to the damp pavement. I bent and dropped them again, a shriek of frustration welling inside me and escaping as a sleep-deprived laugh. So I was tired. Soon, my aunt and surrogate mother would be home in her favorite chair and deep in her history books. And if the humidity and mountains seemed oppressive today, that was a price I gladly paid to live in the fairytale Sierra foothills.

Unlocking my car, I tumbled inside and leaned my head against the rest. The dash clock read five o'clock. Fumbling, I jammed my keys into the ignition and turned them.

Nothing.

I turned the keys again.

Silence.

I banged my head on the steering wheel. If I believed in messages from the universe (and I did), the cosmos would be hinting I was in no condition to drive.

Something thunked and scrabbled on the hood of my car.

I jerked my head upward and was nose to beak with the crow, on the other side of the glass. It squawked, giving me a view of its dark throat, streaked with pink.

"Fine," I grumbled. "I'll call Jayce."

I excavated my cell phone from my purse and called my sister. A coffee shop owner, she'd be awake, prepping for the morning crowd.

"Mmph. Karin?" Jayce's voice was muzzy, no doubt a byproduct of staying out all night at the local bar.

I tamped down my rising irritation. It wasn't Jayce's fault my car wasn't working, and I had no social life. "Yeah," I said. "Are you okay?"

"Ugh. Hangover. Headache." My sister groaned. "What's wrong? Is Ellen all right?"

"We're at the hospital. They're keeping her for observation."

"Again?" Jayce sighed. "What did they say? It's not serious, is it?"

"Another infection, they think. Can you come get me? I didn't get any sleep, and I don't think I'm safe to drive. Plus, my battery's dead."

"Are you being literal or figurative?"

I yawned, jaw cracking, ears popping. "Both."

"Aye, aye Captain. I'll be there in twenty."

I rolled my eyes. My sisters had called me "Captain" since we were six. By birth order, Jayce should have been the bossy, responsible sister. But she, Lenore and I were triplets, three Scorpios born exactly three minutes apart. Traditional birth-order traits did not apply.

Jayce, the oldest and the wild child, had never been able to resist a good sin. Lenore, the youngest, was a bookish introvert. I was the middle child, a worrier by age five who imagined disaster whenever Jayce played in the forest alone, who spent sleepless nights in fear of losing my aunt as we'd lost our parents. And so I'd ordered our childhood lives for stability, making sure homework was done, excursions were planned down to the minute, and clothing was laid out the night before.

The nickname had been the first seeds of my sisters' rebellion, a full-fledged sibling revolution by the time we were ten. I couldn't blame Lenore and Jayce. I'd been a tyrant, and tyrants must be overthrown. But our old patterns hadn't completely died, and Jayce's good-time girl persona just made me crankier.

"Thanks," I said. "I'm parked at the edge of the lot, on the west side. I'll be napping in my car."

She laughed. "Tight squeeze. Good luck with that."

We hung up, and I locked myself in the car and closed my eyes, drifting.

Someone banged on the window.

I bolted upright, banged my knee on the wheel, and yelped in pain.

Jayce grinned through the glass, her long, brunette hair swinging past her shoulders. She wore a painted-on ruby-colored top and jeans. With eyes the color of spring ivy and a heart-shaped face, she looked completely unlike me and Lenore. But though our features varied, strangers who saw us together pegged us for triplets. Our mannerisms, I guess.

I didn't want to guess what I looked like. But I suspected my night at the hospital had drained the color from my already pale skin, turned my long, auburn hair lank. It wasn't fair. Jayce had been out all night having fun and was as fresh as if she'd come from a lazy Saturday sleep-in. It would piss me off if she wasn't my sister.

Rubbing my knee, I checked the dash. The dashboard clock read five thirty. Jayce hadn't wasted any time.

I dragged myself into my sister's F-150. She started the truck, its engine a wolf-like growl, and we drove onto the mountain highway to Doyle.

The rain that had threatened broke loose. First a few fat drops splattering the windshield, then a torrent, washing the truck and the highway clean. The sky darkened, and she flipped on the headlights. We raced, too fast, down the winding road, the pickup's tires screeching as we rounded a tight bend.

Pines big enough to wrap a pickup around flashed past, and I clenched the door handle. "I'm pretty sure the speed limit is thirty-five."

"That's a recommendation, not a rule." Jayce tossed her hair. "I'm thinking of installing tablets in Ground — not at every table, just the high ones. What do you think?"

I double-checked my seat belt and yawned. "I think I'm so tired, my brain itches."

"So, *no* to tableside tablets?"

The windshield wipers beat a hypnotic, squeak-thunk rhythm, and I fought to keep my eyes open. "Let me guess," I said dryly. "You met an engineer in the bar last night?"

"Two venture capitalists from Silicon Valley. Ace and his friend Jack."

"Were you drinking with a deck of cards?"

Her green eyes sparkled. "Only the jokers."

"I take it it wasn't love."

"Not even lust. Well, maybe a little bit of lust. We might have made out."

"*We*? You and both of them?"

Jayce angled her head, frowning. "Why are we all still single?"

"Seriously. Both?" I hadn't been on a date since last year. Doyle was a small town, and options were limited. But that never stopped Jayce from having a good time. Sometimes too good a time.

"Seriously," she said. "Why?"

"Because you want to date everyone, Lenore wants to date no one, and the man I want to date doesn't exist." Was it too much to ask for a take-charge, masculine sort of guy who wasn't a jerk face? They had to exist somewhere.

"Your problem is you and Lenore spend too much time in your heads. And I don't want to date *everyone*. I only want to sample before settling. Is that so wrong?"

"There's a difference between sampling and an all-you-can-eat buffet."

"Meow."

I grinned. "Guilty. I am jealous." My stomach rumbled. "And now I'm hungry." Through half-lidded eyes, I watched the old-timey wood and brick buildings drift slowly past. Water cascaded down the passenger window, blurring the street. I imagined the paved road turning to dirt, the cars turned to carriages, gold miners driving mules down Main Street.

But it was never hard to step back in time in Doyle. The past was always present, and over the last century, the town council had made sure things stayed the same. Mostly. The town was Norman Rockwell meets wi-fi.

"I'm running late," Jayce said. "Mind if I take you to my apartment? You can sleep in the spare room, and later, me or one of the staff can drive you to your car. And there's food in the fridge."

I yawned, my jaw cracking. "That would be great. Thanks. How can you be so awake after partying all night?"

"Beats me. I've got this weird, fizzing feeling. Like something's about to happen." My sister pulled into the alley behind Ground and parked. "And my feelings are never wrong."

I followed her to the rear entrance. The wall's vanilla-colored paint flaked away, revealing rough, red brick. A wooden, exterior stair-case climbed the two-story building to Jayce's apartment. The stairs switch-backed up to a metal door, a winding path to Rapunzel's tower.

She dug in her macramé purse for the keys.

The rain, like me, was warm and dripping. The summer storm should have brought relief from the heat, but it only made the morning more oppressive. Dying to be horizontal, I braced one hand against the damp brickwork and sheltered beneath the awning. The pink scar on my palm — a long-ago spider bite — burned. I rubbed it and winced.

Beneath the stairs, a garbage can lid rattled. A long-haired man in a ragbag of stained and torn clothing set the lid down, his hands shaking.

I touched my sister's arm.

Jayce glanced toward the homeless man. "Hi," she said, cheerful.

He looked at us and froze. Against his hollow, dirt-stained face, his blue eyes blazed, startling.

"Come on in." Jayce turned the key in the latch. The door scraped across the linoleum floor of the darkened kitchen and stuck. "I've got plenty of food and coffee. My treat."

The man stared at Jayce, but most men did. It was a part of her magic, of earth and sex and sky. And it didn't hurt that her clothing never left much to the imagination.

I sighed. My magic was of a more practical bent, bound into knots and knits. It lacked the glamour of Jayce's love spells and the drama of Lenore's mediumship, but my practical magic came in handy. Magic was the only possible explanation for the romance novels I wrote on the side selling as well as they did.

The homeless man ducked and skittered down the alley, his footsteps echoing. His filthy gray coat flapped behind him like wings, as if he were about to launch himself into the sky. He disappeared behind the corner.

"He'll be back when he's ready." Jayce rammed her bare shoulder against the unyielding door. It wrenched open with a metallic squeal. "Did the hospital say when we can visit Ellen?"

Yawning, I raked my fingers through my hair and followed her inside the narrow kitchen. "They said they'd have the test results by eleven, but we can visit her any time." I shivered in the air conditioning and hitched my over-sized purse up my shoulder. The cool air coiled around me, sticking my jeans and now nearly sheer white top unpleasantly to my skin.

"You could have called me," Jayce said. "I'd have gone with you to the hospital." She flipped on the lights. The kitchen was modern, with gleaming metal counter tops and a state-of-the-art dishwasher.

I forced a smile through my exhaustion. "Then we both would have been useless today." We took turns spending nights with our aunt for exactly this reason. Every other week it seemed we were at the hospital. I wasn't sure how long we could go on like this. Ellen *had* to get better soon. I didn't know if her illness had affected her magic, or if it was simply beyond it. In either case, her magic wasn't holding it at bay. Neither were Jayce's potions or Lenore's shamanic journeys, and I'd never had any healing talent.

Fortunately, my practice as a business and estate attorney was light, so light I could moonlight as a romance writer. It was easy to schedule appointments for the afternoons, when I was more awake after a night spent with our aunt. And my writing happened in my spare time. Since I hadn't had a date in forever, I had a lot of spare time.

"Have you called Lenore?" Jayce asked.

"No. It's too early, and there's nothing we can do. I'll call Lenore when I wake up, unless you want to do the honors." The bookstore where our other sister worked didn't open until noon, and Lenore was a late riser.

"No. You talked to the doctors. She'll want to hear it from you."

Another jaw-snapping yawn, and I mounted the stairs. "Guest bed?"

"You know the way."

Halfway up the stairs, I paused. The atmosphere felt odd, off. The coldness of the A/C had the chill of a morgue, and in my mind's eye I saw a metal table in a tiled room, and the shape of a woman's form beneath a white sheet.

I shook my head, ridding myself of the vision I'd conjured. My writerly imagination worked best when I hovered between sleep and wakefulness, as I was now. But I didn't want to imagine or write, I wanted to sleep, and I continued up the stairs. The toe of my Mary Jane caught on the last step, and I nearly tumbled, face first, onto the kilim rug covering the distressed wood floor.

Go back.

Startled, I looked toward the white-painted, brick alcove, where ivy framed the space above a couch. Nobody was there.

We've all got voices in our heads (I think). Call them angels or intuition, madness or ego. In the past I'd had feelings — whispers of a truth. But this time, this voice, sounded as if it had been shouted in my left ear.

I rubbed my neck and glanced into Jayce's open bedroom. The bed was unmade, patterned throw pillows jumbled across it, an open magazine on the floor. I walked toward the peeling, white door to the tiny guest room.

Head cocked, listening, I didn't notice the discarded, stiletto heel. I stepped on it and cursed. In Jayce's place, stray stilettos were par for the course, and I should have been more watchful.

But a knot, tight and untidy, formed in my chest.

Something was wrong.

My heart thumped too fast, and I turned, suddenly wide awake.

My sister screamed.

"Jayce!" I thundered down the wooden stairs and pinballed off a wall, my ankle twisting on the final step into the kitchen.

"Here," she choked out. "Oh, God."

I brushed past the brown and gray, ikat-patterned curtain into the café.

Jayce stood on the customer side of the dark-wood counter and stared at a low table.

I took another step inside the room. Its natural brick walls, lined with paintings and rugs, seemed to have pulled in a damp chill from the air conditioning and amplified it. A spider plant hanging above the counter was swinging. Jayce gripped a watering can to her chest.

"What is it?" I asked. "What's wrong? Not another mouse?" Jayce hated mice, but she refused to kill them, instituting a catch-and-release program. And anybody but Jayce was in charge of the catch.

She tore her gaze from the table. "She's dead."

I lurched sideways, the life force draining from my body. Not Ellen. Not yet. Not now. Our aunt had cared for us since our mom had died in childbirth, and our dad had died... Not Ellen. Icicles pierced my heart. "Ellen?" I whispered.

"Alicia. Alicia Duarte." Jayce's voice cracked. "She's dead."

"What?" Whipping around the counter, I came to stand beside my sister. I stared.

The newspaper editor Alicia Duarte lay on the floor between a wooden table and two, brown-cushioned chairs. Blood pooled beneath her blond head on the bamboo floor. Her eyes stared, blank, at the ceiling. For a wild moment I believed she wasn't real. It was a trick. The body was wax. I was dreaming.

My stomach rolled, sluggish. Someone had done this to her. I scanned the café, my breath coming short and fast, but we were alone.

Shocked, I looked to my sister. Jayce's green eyes were wide, her forehead damp in spite of the arctic air conditioning. But there was something else in her gaze.

Guilt.

That snapped me out of my fear. What was Alicia Duarte doing in my sister's café? "Why is she dead?" It was a stupid question, but my brain and my mouth seemed disconnected.

"How should I know why she's dead?"

"She's in Ground! Why is she in your coffee shop?"

"I don't know!" Jayce clapped her hand over her mouth. "Oh, God. Alicia." She fumbled her way to a chair and sat, gripping the watering can.

Movements stilted, I walked to the wall phone behind the counter and dialed the police.

"Nine-one-one, what is your emergency?"

"This is Karin Bonheim. I'm at Ground Café on Main Street. We've found a dead woman." The front entrance didn't appear broken into. Its red-framed windows were intact. And the rear kitchen door had been locked. How the hell had Alicia gotten inside the closed café?

The dispatcher squawked into the receiver, and I hung up the phone. My stomach rolled. Jayce's look of guilt... I'd seen it too many times to mistake it, though I hadn't seen it often in the last few years. Jayce had outgrown that particular emotion.

I bit my lower lip. It was no secret Jayce was better friends with Alicia's husband, Brayden, than with Alicia. Could Jayce have given Brayden a key? Had he come here, and then his wife somehow... And there'd been an argument...

I swallowed. Whatever had happened, my sister couldn't have been involved.

But why was Alicia's body here?

Click here to get your copy of *Bound* and can keep reading this magical series today!

More Kirsten Weiss

THE DOYLE WITCH MYSTERIES

In a mountain town where magic lies hidden in its foundations and forests, three witchy sisters must master their powers and shatter a curse before it destroys them and the home they love.

This thrilling witch mystery series is perfect for fans of Annabel Chase, Adele Abbot, and Amanda Lee. If you love stories rich with packed with magic, mystery, and murder, you'll love the Witches of Doyle. Follow the magic with the Doyle Witch trilogy, starting with book 1, *Bound*.

The Mystery School Series

The Doyle Witches have created a mystery school, and a woman starting over becomes a student of magic and murder...

This metaphysical mystery series is perfect for readers who love a good page-turner as well as the deeper questions that accompany life's transitions. These empowering books come with their own oracle app, the UnTarot, plus downloadable mystery school worksheets. The Doyle Witch magic continues, starting with book 1, *Legacy of the Witch*.

The Perfectly Proper Paranormal Museum Mysteries

When highflying Maddie Kosloski is railroaded into managing her small-town's paranormal museum, she tells herself it's only temporary... until a corpse in the museum embroils her in murders past and present.

If you love quirky characters and cats with attitude, you'll love this laugh-out-loud cozy mystery series with a light paranormal twist. It's perfect for fans of Jana DeLeon, Laura Childs, and Juliet Blackwell. Start with book 1, *The Perfectly Proper Paranormal Museum*, and experience these charming wine-country whodunits today.

The Tea & Tarot Cozy Mysteries

Welcome to Beanblossom's Tea and Tarot, where each and every cozy mystery brews up hilarious trouble.

Abigail Beanblossom's dream of owning a tearoom is about to come true. She's got the lease, the start-up funds, and the recipes. But Abigail's out of a tearoom and into hot water when her realtor turns out to be a conman... and then turns up dead.

Take a whimsical journey with Abigail and her partner Hyperion through the seaside town of San Borromeo (patron saint of heartburn sufferers). And be sure to check out the easy tearoom recipes in the back of each book! Start the adventure with book 1, *Steeped in Murder*.

The Wits' End Cozy Mysteries

Cozy mysteries that are out of this world...

Running the best little UFO-themed B&B in the Sierras takes organization, breakfasting chops, and a talent for turning up trouble.

The truth is out there... Way out there in these hilarious whodunits. Start the series and beam up book 1, *At Wits' End*, today!

Pie Town Cozy Mysteries

When Val followed her fiancé to coastal San Nicholas, she had ambitions of starting a new life and a pie shop. One broken engagement later, at least her dream of opening a pie shop has come true.... Until one of her regulars keels over at the counter.

Welcome to Pie Town, where Val and pie-crust specialist Charlene are baking up hilarious trouble. Start this laugh-out-loud cozy mystery series with book 1, *The Quiche and the Dead*.

A Big Murder Mystery Series

Small Town. Big Murder.

The number one secret to my success as a bodyguard? Staying under the radar. But when a wildly public disaster blew up my career and reputation, it turned my perfect, solitary life upside down.

I thought my tiny hometown of Nowhere would be the ideal out-of-the-way refuge to wait out the media storm.

It wasn't.

My little brother had moved into a treehouse. The obscure mountain town had decided to attract tourists with the world's largest collection of big things... Yes, Nowhere now has the world's largest pizza cutter. And lawn flamingo. And ball of yarn...

And then I stumbled over a dead body.

All the evidence points to my brother being the bad guy. I may have been out of his life for a while—okay, five years—but I know he's no killer. Can I clear my brother before he becomes Nowhere's next Big Fatality?

A fast-paced and funny cozy mystery series, start with Big Shot.

The Riga Hayworth Paranormal Mysteries

Her gargoyle's got an attitude.

Her magic's on the blink.

Alchemy might be the cure... if Riga can survive long enough to puzzle out its mysteries.

All Riga wants is to solve her own personal mystery—how to rebuild her magical life. But her new talent for unearthing murder keeps getting in the way...

If you're looking for a magical page-turner with a complicated, 40-something heroine, read the paranormal mystery series that fans of Patricia Briggs and Ilona Andrews call AMAZING! Start your next adventure with book 1, *The Alchemical Detective*.

Sensibility Grey Steampunk Suspense

California Territory, 1848.

Steam-powered technology is still in its infancy.

Gold has been discovered, emptying the village of San Francisco of its male population.

And newly arrived immigrant, Englishwoman Sensibility Grey, is alone.

The territory may hold more dangers than Sensibility can manage. Pursued by government agents and a secret society, Sensibility must decipher her father's clockwork secrets, before time runs out.

If you love over-the-top characters, twisty mysteries, and complicated heroines, you'll love the Sensibility Grey series of steampunk suspense. Start this steampunk adventure with book 1, *Steam and Sensibility*.

Connect with Kirsten

Sign up for my newsletter and get a special digital prize pack for joining, including an exclusive Tea & Tarot novella, *Fortune Favors the Grave*.
https://kirstenweiss.com
Or maybe you'd like to chat with other whimsical mystery fans? Come join Kirsten's reader page on Facebook:
https://www.facebook.com/kirsten.weiss
Or... sign up for my read and review team on Booksprout:
https://booksprout.co/author/8142/kirsten-weiss

About the Author

I BELIEVE IN FREE-WILL, and that we all can make a difference. I believe that beauty blossoms in the conscious life, particularly with friends, family, and strangers. I believe that genre fiction has become generic, and it doesn't have to be.

My current focus is my new Mystery School series, starting with *Legacy of the Witch*. Traditionally, women's fiction refers to fiction where a woman—usually in her midlife—is going through some sort of dramatic change. A lot of us do go through big transitions in midlife. We get divorced or remarried. The kids leave the nest. Our bodies change. The midlife crisis is real—though it manifests in different ways—as we look back on where we've been, where we're going, and the time we have left.

Now in my mid-fifties, I've spent more time thinking about the big "meaning of life" issues. It seemed like approaching those issues through witch fiction, and through a fictional mystery school, would be a fun and a useful way for me to work out some of these ideas in my own head—about change and letting go, faith and fear, and love and longing.

After growing up on a diet of Nancy Drew, Sherlock Holmes, and Agatha Christie, I've published over 60 mysteries—from cozies to supernatural suspense, as well as an experimental fiction book on Tarot. Spending over 20 years working overseas in international development, I learned that perception is not reality, and things are often not what they seem—for better or worse.

There isn't a winter holiday or a type of chocolate I don't love, and some of my best friends are fictional.

Sign up for my **newsletter** for exclusive stories and book updates. I also have a read-and-review tea via **Booksprout** and I'm looking for honest and thoughtful reviews! If you're interested, download the **Booksprout app**, follow me on Booksprout, and opt-in for email notifications.

BB   bookbub.com/profile/kirsten-weiss

g   goodreads.com/author/show/5346143.Kirsten_Weiss

f   facebook.com/kirsten.weiss

O   instagram.com/kirstenweissauthor/

▶   youtube.com/@KirstenWeiss-Writer?sub_confirmation=1

Other misterio press books

Please check out these other great *misterio press* series:
Karma's A Bitch: Pet Psychic Mysteries
by Shannon Esposito
Multiple Motives: Kate Huntington Mysteries
by Kassandra Lamb
The Metaphysical Detective: Riga Hayworth Paranormal
Mysteries
by Kirsten Weiss
Dangerous
and Unseemly: Concordia Wells Historical Mysteries
by K.B. Owen
Murder, Honey: Carol Sabala Mysteries
by Vinnie Hansen
Payback: Unintended Consequences Romantic Suspense
by Jessica Dale
Buried in the Dark: Frankie O'Farrell Mysteries
by Shannon Esposito
To Kill A Labrador: Marcia Banks and Buddy Cozy Mysteries
by Kassandra Lamb
Lethal Assumptions: C.o.P. on the Scene Mysteries
by Kassandra Lamb
Never
Sleep: Chronicles of a Lady Detective Historical Mysteries
by K.B. Owen
Bound: Witches of Doyle Cozy Mysteries
by Kirsten Weiss

At Wits' End Doyle Cozy Mysteries

by Kirsten Weiss

Steeped In Murder: Tea and Tarot Mysteries

by Kirsten Weiss

The Perfectly Proper Paranormal Museum Mysteries

by Kirsten Weiss

Big

Shot: The Big Murder Mysteries

by Kirsten Weiss

Steam and Sensibility: Sensibility Grey Steampunk Mysteries

by Kirsten Weiss

Full

Mortality: Nikki Latrelle Mysteries

by Sasscer Hill

ChainLinked: Moccasin Cove Mysteries

by Liz Boeger

Maui Widow Waltz: Islands of Aloha Mysteries

by JoAnn Bassett

Plus even more great mysteries/thrillers in the *misterio press* bookstore

Manufactured by Amazon.ca
Acheson, AB